James O. Halliwell-Phillipps

The Stratford Records and the Shakespeare Autotypes

to which is prefixed the farewell of the oldest living Shakespearean

biographer to the Shakespeare-councils

James O. Halliwell-Phillipps

The Stratford Records and the Shakespeare Autotypes
to which is prefixed the farewell of the oldest living Shakespearean biographer to the Shakespeare-councils

ISBN/EAN: 9783337093044

Printed in Europe, USA, Canada, Australia, Japan

Cover: Foto ©Andreas Hilbeck / pixelio.de

More available books at **www.hansebooks.com**

THE STRATFORD RECORDS

AND

THE SHAKESPEARE AUTOTYPES.

FIFTH EDITION.

What has become, said Giafar, of the old philosopher Abdallah, who was so often, when I was last here, in the Sultan's green-house, and who taught me the virtues of herbs? You are not likely to see him there again, said Nourreddin. When he arrived,—it was in the reign of Camalralzaman, long, long ago,—one saw nothing in the green-house but what looked like one of those dirt-heaps, covered with weeds and fragments of jars, that are so common on the banks of the Ganges. Now after Abdallah had spent a life-time of Hindbad in reclaiming the plants, the Sultan made a new grand-vizier, who did not even know one of their names, ruler of the green-house, and,—O Allah! you will hardly believe me,—the new grand-vizier told the people that Abdallah had committed a very wicked act, that he had moved a row of pots into the sun-light for nearly an hour, and that he deserved to be bastinadoed. This was too much for the old philosopher, who had worked like a slave for so many years, and had never asked for a cowry. So Abdallah left the Palace in disgust, and, if you want to see him, you must go to his mountain-home in the province of Balsula, where he has a green-house as large as the Sultan's, and where there are no grand-viziers. By Allah, said Giafar, he will be a bull-calf if he works any more for the Sultan.—*Tales from the Arabic, Literally Translated*, ed. 1837, p. 97.

THE STRATFORD RECORDS

AND THE

SHAKESPEARE AUTOTYPES.

THE FIFTH EDITION.

---

*To which is Prefixed the Farewell of the oldest living
Shakespearean Biographer to the Shakespeare-Councils
of the Town which should be, but which is not, the
chosen Centre of Shakespeare-Biographical
Research.*

AND FOR YOUR (PALEOGRAPHICAL) WRITING AND READING, LET
THAT APPEAR WHEN THERE IS NO NEED OF SUCH VANITY.
                              MUCH ADO ABOUT NOTHING.

LONDON:

HARRISON AND SONS, No. 59, PALL MALL.

1887.

LONDON :

HARRISON AND SONS, PRINTERS IN ORDINARY TO HER MAJESTY,
ST. MARTIN'S LANE.

PREFACE.

The reasons that have led to my retirement from the Shakespearean councils of Stratford-on-Avon having, I find, been greatly misunderstood, an endeavour must be made to give a more extended publicity to the true causes. A large number of copies of this pamphlet will, therefore, be distributed gratuitously, and it will also be accessible to the general public.

My dispute is not with the people of Stratford. Every surviving old or intimate friend that I ever had there is still my old or intimate friend, and I have every reason to believe that I am only out of favour with the members of an imperious little oligarchy, who resent the slightest question of their supremacy, and who consider it highly indecorous that so inferior a being as a Shakespearean biographer should venture to dispute the validity of their decrees.

I would have put up with almost anything could I have seen that the members of that oligarchy had taken a real interest in the evidences of ancient Stratford, but so far from this being the case, there are abundant indications that they do not in their hearts care one single halfpenny about them. If the reader will turn to what is said at pp. 39–49, and especially to pp. 43–49, he must perforce acknowledge that a more complete exposure of the hypocritical display of a pseudo-enthusiasm was never submitted to the public.

It would have been better if there had been merely indifference, if the ancient Shakespeare memorials had been quietly let alone; but this unfortunately is not the case. Those memorials are being tampered with in all directions. Thus, for example, the main interest of the gardens at New Place rests in the exact preservation of Shakespeare's own boundaries; but an adjoining footpath was thought to be too narrow, and so a slice of the poet's garden has been divorced from its associations and transferred to Chapel Lane. The same spirit, that in which the integrity of relics of the past is habitually sacrificed to provincial notions of expediency, has prevailed in the direction of the recent operations at the Church. Not the slightest trouble was taken to make a preliminary investigation into the history* of its

---

* During the execrable "restoration" of the Church in 1835 the remains of St. Thomas's Chapel, one of its most interesting adjuncts, were ruthlessly discarded. A considerable portion of those remains came into my possession many years ago, and I gave them to the then Vicar in the hope that they would be replaced, but they were consigned instead to a corner of the churchyard. Interesting materials for the history of the Chapel are preserved both at Stratford and in our national Record Office.

architectural details, and, as clearly appears from the story of the Hart tablet, there was not even a schedule drawn up of the objects that demanded careful preservation. The anticipated effect upon modern eyes appears to have been the only motive power. Owning myself by far the largest collection of drawings of the Church that has ever been brought together, including some of the earliest known to exist, I thought it my duty, in a letter to Sir Arthur Hodgson, to offer the Committee the use of them ; but a polite acknowledgment of the letter was all that emanated from the offer, and it was not of course my province to pursue the matter further.

The proceedings of the oligarchy in all literary matters connected with the town have been of the most ludicrous description. For some inscrutable reason they all at once made a terrific fuss about their medieval records, so much so that " your Committee," who did not pretend to be able to read them, presented an elaborate report on their extreme value and importance to Sir Arthur Hodgson, who was in a similar predicament, both, however, agreeing that the meetings at the Town Hall would be considerably more effective if held in the stimulating presence of two or three of these fascinating hieroglyphics. The selection must have been easily made if others shared Sir Arthur's opinion (see pp. 93, 94) that one ancient document was quite as good as another for all practical purposes. It was perhaps this persuasion that induced the oligarchy to allow me last year, at a public auction and in the presence of their own accredited agent, to secure sixty-six medieval records, all relating to Stratford-on-Avon and its immediate neighbourhood, and all equally at least if not more valuable than those in possession of the town, at the rate of sixteen-pence a-piece! This startling result was certainly not due to any favourable consideration towards myself, for I was not present, and no one at the sale knew who was the real purchaser, the biddings having been made by a friend and in his own name.

Stratford-on-Avon, under the management of its oligarchy, instead of being, as it ought to be, the centre of Shakespeare-biographical research, has become the seat of Shakespearean charlatanry. There are no end of Shakespearean speechifyings, Shakespearean platitudes, drums and trumpets, flags and banners, and before long no doubt some kind of repetition of Garrick's jubilee tomfoolery. But it is in vain to look to its oligarchy for the dissemination of really effective Shakespeare work. This appears beyond dispute in the lamentably meagre reports that they present,—only once in a year, recollect,—to the trustees of Shakespeare's Birth-Place. Thus we are told that two hundred old deeds have been presented, but not a word as to their contents, or even as to their dates, or even as to the special localities to which they relate. They could find plenty of time last year to stick their pins and needles into me, but not leisure to furnish the trustees with so many as twenty lines in which to record their proceedings for an entire twelvemonth, nor a spare day to frame a section on the new evidences that had then recently appeared respecting the integrity of the national memorial which is practically under their care. Then, again, why is Mr. Warner's catalogue of their rarities suffered to remain in manuscript, instead of being printed for the use of Shakespearean scholars? All this is in striking contrast to the enlightened liberality shown by the Governors of Dulwich College in respect to another of Mr. Warner's admirable calendars.

As to myself, personally, I will defy the Stratford oligarchy to produce a single instance in which I have been deserving of censure in

my work as Stratford's honorary servant, or to
show that my offence is deeper than in resist-
ance to the pressure of an arrogant despotism.
Grotesquely arrogant it is true, but yet with a
sufficiency of the vulgarity of condescension to
render it unpalatable. There has been no real
desire on their part to effect a reconciliation on
terms that a person of independent character
could accept. There has been no withdrawal of
the insolent letters and speeches. No apology
has been made for the impertinent falsehood
respecting me which is exposed at pp. 95–96.
No steps have been taken by the Council to
neutralize the unwarrantable observations that
have been uttered in their presence. The only
overture for peace that they have made consisted of a quasi-official invitation that I received
a few months ago to partake of the Mayor's
hospitality on the occasion of my anticipated
attendance at a Shakespearean meeting, but
an acceptance of that invitation would, to my
thinking, have been tantamount to an acknowledgment that I had deserved the ungentlemanly criticisms to which I had been
subjected.

Since this last sentence has been written
another invitation of a similar character has
been received from Sir Arthur Hodgson, but

what in the world is the use of these little bits
of politeness when no other attempt is made to
efface the recollection of a series of insults ?
The practical illustration of the pretty little
allegorical overture,—" Come into my parlour,
says the spider to the fly,"—may perhaps be
very well once in a way, but it is apt to pall on
repetition. Even Justice Shallow himself would
not have been so simple as to have taken the
part of Sir Dagonet in Arthur's Show if he had
been previously sat upon by the other per-
formers ; and surely no reasonable being can be
surprised at my absence from the pageant or at
my having had quite enough of its surroundings.

It should be mentioned that the fourth
edition of this pamphlet, which was ready
for delivery nearly a year ago, was rigidly
suppressed through the belief, shared with a
Stratford friend, that a door could be opened
for the restoration of harmony. We neither of
us spared any efforts in furtherance of that
object, while on my part I made concessions
that landed me too dangerously near the
verge of humiliation,—concessions that were
erroneously interpreted, as they so often are
in cases of this kind, into a confession that I
was anxious for peace at any price. Thus it
happened that an ultra-generous scheme that

I had devised for reconciliation was trifled with month after month, and I felt that I should be placing myself in an obsequious and embarrassing position if I continued to sanction its validity. I had fortunately made an express stipulation that time, to use a legal phrase, was to be the essence of the contract, a condition under which I have withdrawn for ever all the proposed concessions, and my future visits to Stratford, so long to me a second home, will be those of an independent critic.

I must now conclude with a farewell, but in taking leave of gentlemen with whose predecessors I worked for nearly forty years in unbroken harmony, and in withdrawing altogether from further participation in the work or deliberations of the present Shakespearean councils of Stratford-on-Avon, it is impossible not to cast a "long lingering look behind" upon the many happy days I have erewhile passed in Shakespeare's town, days in which courtesy asserted its even sway and in which dictatorial impertinences were unknown.

J. O. HALLIWELL-PHILLIPPS.

Hollingbury Copse, Brighton.
October, 1887.

PREFACE TO THE FOURTH EDITION.

Since the last edition of this little brochure was issued I have come across a number of letters from Mr. W. O. Hunt, the late town-clerk of Stratford-on-Avon, some of them dated so far back as the year 1847, and they throw so clear a light on more than one point in dispute that I am tempted to introduce a few extracts from them in the following pages, all being of a sufficiently quasi-official character to justify their publication.

It is a pity that there should be a necessity for the continuance of that which is, apart from personal considerations, at least an unprofitable if not a deleterious controversy, as well as one of no general interest; but I am not inclined to pass over altogether without remonstrance the persistent efforts made by a little coterie to darken the character of my Stratford work by injurious misrepresentations. Not a word on the subject would ever have been heard from me had they contented themselves with simply ignoring my many years of patient labour as unworthy of either notice or regard, but it is a different matter when they have led the public to infer that my work was based on narrow and selfish designs, and when, as at the very last meeting of the Trustees, it is insinuated that it has not been conscientiously executed. Refutation can hardly in such a case be fairly considered the result of an undue sensitiveness. It is no light matter for a person who has been intimately connected with a town for considerably upwards of thirty years without exchanging a cross word with any one, and where all his old friends whom death has spared are still his old friends, to be not only involved in conflict with its present leading citizens, but prejudiced by the dissemination of ex parte versions of the origin and subsequent history of the dissension. To those old friends, and to lovers of fair-play in Shakespearean matters, these pages are addressed.

Apart from the unexpected estimate of my work there were unfortunate misunderstandings that should long since have been amicably closed instead of being still under review. The latter result is due to amusing and frantic attempts on the part of my opponents to enforce me into an abject surrender, an object that has underlaid every movement. So when I did everything in my power, even to the condonation of most serious discourtesies (see

p. 70), to restore harmony, the same individual,
—a gentleman of paramount influence in all
the affairs of the town,—who then cordially
supported my efforts, and who had only just
previously formally seconded at a Council
meeting a friendly and complimentary resolution in my favour, organised immediately afterwards a local attack upon me in another
direction. These erratic proceedings landed
us into this exceedingly curious position,—
we were to be sworn-brothers in the Record-
Room and simultaneously at loggerheads in
the adjoining Birth-Place ; conditions under
which anything like pleasant or effective work
was out of the question, and my retirement
followed as a matter of course. It was clear,
moreover, that a real desire for an equitable
peace was restricted to myself. I am, indeed,
always ready in any controversy to "show my
valour and put up my sword," whenever I
can do so on any kind of reasonable terms,
but, in the present instance, although in the
course of so lengthened a dispute faults have
no doubt been committed on both sides, I must
take the liberty, until there is a reversal of
the singularly unfair policy that I have hitherto
encountered, of considering myself entitled to
act on the defensive.

Although such a reversal would not now affect my determination to withdraw altogether from Stratford work,—work that, at my advanced age, would under any circumstances have been transferred before long to younger men,—it might perhaps lead to the termination of a deplorable controversy for which there can be no real compensation even in victory. No one would rejoice more than myself at such a result,—no one more anxious to repair to the utmost of my power any action in which it may be generally considered by independent observers that I have been to blame,—but all this must, if necessary, be incident to the continued refutation, through the evidence of established facts, of the indefensible and ungracious attacks to which I have been and am still being subjected.

J. O. HALLIWELL-PHILLIPPS.

Hollingbury Copse, Brighton.
October the 25th, 1886.

PREFACE TO THE FIRST EDITION.

Singular misconceptions being prevalent at Stratford respecting my record-work and the treatment that I have met with in that town, I am tempted to devote a few pages to the subject; and the rather as those delusions have lately assumed a definite form and made a public appearance in the columns of an important local journal. The following, for example, is the commencement of a recent leading article in the Stratford-on-Avon Herald, a newspaper which has a large circulation in the town and neighbourhood,—

The Stratford Corporation are in possession of many very interesting records extending from the earliest times, but it is only recently that the value of these documents has dawned upon the Corporate mind. They were permitted to lie in the muniment-room at the Birthplace unclassified, uncalendared, uncared for, and this indifference to their existence, had it continued, would have led ultimately to their decay, and consequent loss to the town. A little time ago attention was directed to the condition of these records, and the Corporation was prevailed upon to appoint a committee to superintend their classification and calendaring. Mr. Hardy, a gentleman in every way qualified for the work, was entrusted with the task of reducing these records from their chaotic state to something like order, and it is admitted that, so far as the work has proceeded, he has admirably discharged his duty. Of course gentlemen endowed with special talent of this kind require adequate payment for their services, and already Mr. Hardy's account amounts to one hundred and eighty pounds.

A few days previously the Chairman of the local Record Committee, speaking of course with authority, informed the Council, referring to the unbound records of the Guild, that "they were now gradually decaying and losing their value."

If these allegations are correct, then it follows that I have grossly neglected my duty in a work undertaken for a Corporation that did me the honour some years ago to entrust me with the arrangement of their records. How far the implied accusations are correct will be gathered by the public from the statements that follow.

Then, again, the Stratford Herald, in another recent leader, observes,—

This can be said *from our own knowledge* that Mr. Halliwell-Phillipps has been treated *with the greatest courtesy* by the Stratford Corporation *and by every individual member of it;* and that, if he thinks this treatment has not been extended to him, his mind has received a particular bias from people whose mental condition renders them incapable of imparting to him the truth.*

* Whatever can be the real meaning of this extraordinary paragraph? If the notion is that I have been influenced by baseless gossip, then the Stratford Herald has been falling into the identical error it has had the charity to warn me against, or otherwise so unfounded an insinuation would never have found its way into its columns. I may, however, be wrong in this surmise, for there is so much in the article in which the above paragraph occurs which is of so extremely mysterious a character that, as poor Tom Hood used to say of the middle-cut of salmon, it is impossible to make either head or tail of it.

If there is no mistake in the statements that are here italicized, it follows that, after an intimate connexion with Stratford for nearly forty years without exchanging a cross word with anybody, I was suddenly transformed into one of those ungracious old fellows who rush into quarrels without any kind of provocation.

Being naturally reluctant that statements favouring this impression should go forth unchallenged, I have drawn up, in the latter part of this brochure, an explicit account of the circumstances which induced me to believe that I had been vexatiously treated. It is for the public to say, upon a review of those circumstances, if I have arrived at such a conclusion on insufficient grounds, or if I can be fairly represented at Stratford as an imaginative person who sees nothing but discourtesy in the very centre of æsthetic amenities.

Hollingbury Copse, Brighton,
December, 1884.

THE STRATFORD RECORDS.

It is about forty years since I was introduced to the Stratford records. They then and for long afterwards mainly consisted of thousands of separate documents which had been collected into boxes and were therein preserved, the ancient ones tangled with the modern in wild confusion.

A considerable number of the documents had been crumpled and slightly mutilated, but nothing like decay had set in, nor were they in any way in a dangerous state. There was, it is true, no end of dust, but that is an object in a record-room as welcome to the eyes of a paleographer as that of drain-pipes in a clay-field is to a farmer. Records are very rarely injured by dust, whilst its presence is an indication of the absence of moisture, their greatest and most dangerous enemy. If they are placed in a damp room, their ultimate destruction is a question of a single generation, and when once fungi have been permitted to take root unchecked for even a very few years, all the efforts of the most skilful binders in the world will be unable to repair the damage. Here there was nothing of the kind.

But although there was no urgency so far as the safety of the records was concerned, they were in an exceedingly inconvenient condition for literary reference, and the town-clerk—the late Mr. W. O. Hunt—was extremely anxious to have them put into thorough working order. We had several discussions on the subject, but most, if not all of them, concluded with one of his favourite speeches,—" where's the money to come from ?" As the Stratford Herald well remarks, in reference to the engagement of a record-reader, " of course gentlemen endowed with special talent of this kind require adequate payment for their services ;" and, in this case, what with the usual fees, travelling and hotel costs, all necessarily extending over a consider-able period, the records could not possibly have been put into accessible order and calendared under an expenditure which, as Mr. Hunt said over and over again, the Corporation neither would incur, nor would be justified in incurring, for such a purpose.

I cannot recall the precise date,* but some years afterwards I offered to arrange and

* Since this was written I have found the exact date in a letter from Mr. W. O. Hunt, 8 May, 1862, in which he says,—" I read your letter about the Corporation records to the Town Council at their meeting

calendar all the documents from the earliest times to the year 1750 without fee. The offer was at once accepted by the Corporation, the members of whom were in every way most kind and obliging, scarcely a day passing without one or other looking in to see if I wanted anything to render my working more convenient. But there was none of that fussy interference which would have rendered my task an exceedingly disagreeable one. They had the sagacity to be aware that a good and useful work was in hand, and, believing that I knew what I was about, had the good sense to let me do it in my own way. There was, moreover, none of that tiresome intrusion of advice-giving in matters which they had never studied. To the best of my recollection the only question ever put to me respecting the interior of a document was by one of the aldermen, a scientific chemist, who, taking up from the table an ancient demurrer, wished to know which was the right side upwards? This was far better and more sensible of him than attempting to give what must necessarily have been an unsound opinion either on the document itself or on my method of work. It was no more disgrace to my kind

yesterday, and they agreed at once to your suggestions about them, and desired me to offer you their grateful acknowledgments for your liberal offer to calendar them."

friend, the chemist, not being able to decipher an old record than there would have been to me in my owning that I might have poisoned somebody had I made up one of his prescriptions.

The first and most tedious part of my business was to separate the modern and ancient records. When this task had been effected, it appeared that there were no fewer than 5823 separate ancient documents all of which were of course to be arranged and calendared. For reasons that will be presently shown there were 954 of these records which it was not thought expedient to send to the binders. The remaining 4869 records, after each one had been duly numbered and calendared, were confided to Mr. Tuckett, the binder to the British Museum, and who, being in the daily habit of binding manuscripts for the national establishment, was the most efficient person for the task that could have been selected. In Mr. Tuckett's hands every document requiring mending was neatly repaired and the whole were delivered to the Corporation substantially bound in 29 volumes ; ever since which time there is not a single document amongst the 4869 that could not, by the aid of the calendar, be readily found in two or three minutes. It follows, therefore, that my implied shortcomings must be restricted to the above-named 954 documents, and now we shall see upon what grounds such implications can be founded.

The 954 unbound documents consist of,—1. The Town Charters.—2. Expired and surrendered leases.—3. A few miscellaneous documents.—4. The unbound records of the Guild. It will be most convenient to speak of each of these divisions in its order.

1. Every lawyer is aware how extremely imprudent it is to disturb in the minutest degree even the external integrity of original title-deeds, and Mr. Hunt specifically excluded the Charters of Incorporation from binding operations. It was his opinion that the miscellaneous ancient documents were valueless for legal purposes, but that the Town Charters partook of a different character. Although many of their provisions had been abrogated by the Municipal Reform Act, there were some important ones that were still in force, and he thought that if intricate legal questions were to arise on the wording of those charters, as was the case in the seventeenth century in a litigation between the Corporation and the Vicar, it would at all events be advisable, if not essential, that they should be produced before the Court in exactly their original state.

2. Expired and surrendered leases, 719 of which are in the Record Room, are about the least interesting and valuable of all descriptions of records. They are very rarely of any use excepting in the determination of boundaries, and the greater portion of the Stratford collection is exceptionally worthless owing to the descriptions of parcels being generally repeated over and over again in precisely the same terms, even the names of owners of adjoining properties being frequently continued for generations after their respective deaths. Nearly all, if not all, that there can be of positive interest, although the early ones may be occasionally useful for reference, is given in the printed Calendar, pp. 118 to 166; and as all these leases are placed in divisions for each Ward, there is no difficulty in any one accustomed to research finding what may be wanted. They are mostly in exceedingly good condition, and although there are a few that might be the better for repairs, there are none in a state of cumulative decay. Indentures of this kind are, moreover, more expensive and troublesome to bind than the earlier Guild Records, and the repairing and binding of 119 of the latter have just cost the Corporation somewhere about £50. At the same rate the binding of these 719 leases would

have cost £300, and I cannot help thinking that it would have been very thoughtless on my part if, entertaining so strong an opinion as to their very small literary value, I had involved the Corporation in so large an expenditure, or even in a quarter of it, for such an object.

3. About a dozen unbound documents, consisting mainly of rolls, constitutions of local trading companies, &c., all of which were either inconvenient for, or not thought to be worth, binding.

4. The unbound records of the Guild are of a kind that are more easily bound than those last-mentioned, but they are of a class that are seldom enquired after. As to these of Stratford, with the exception of those which relate to the building of the Guild Chapel, there are none of more special interest than that which attaches to thousands of similar guild records in many other towns. There are none of them of the least Shakespeare-biographical value, and they all belong to one of the classes of the Town Records that no Shakespearean student would dream of troubling his head about. They would of course be of use to the county topographer, but of none in any of those branches through the inclusion of which the Stratford Records have attained their chief distinction.

There was no doubt a section of these documents that admitted of repair, but in the absence of the fear of accruing injury, and considering how extremely few were the persons to whom they were of interest, I did not feel myself authorized in putting the Corporation to the expense of having them bound. It is upon a portion, little more than one half, of these unbound guild records that the sum of £180 has recently been expended, viz., £64 by the Corporation, and the remainder, with his usual liberality, by Mr. Charles Flower, the former sum, however, including the cost of framing the Charters of Incorporation. I am glad indeed to find that so much money can now be cheerfully expended at Stratford in such a direction, but I must be allowed to enter a protest against the insinuation that my shortcomings have rendered the outlay a matter of necessity.

I must also be allowed to protest against the insinuation that I surrendered my work into the hands of the Corporation, leaving a number of unbound records in a dangerous and perishing condition. I was neither so careless nor so indifferent to the due execution of the trust that had been confided to me. No mildew had set in,—the rarity of consultation put on one side the question of wear and tear,—and whatever repairs might have been thought acceptable in the luxury of order, there were none that could not have been deferred for an indefinite period without the slightest accruing injury to any of the documents. It must be recollected that I was entrusted with the direction of the binding and repairs, that I was dealing with public money, and that I should not have been justified in involving the Corporation in an expenditure beyond that which was prudently necessary. It was Mr. Hunt's express desire that every reasonable precaution should be taken to limit the cost, and the result was that 4869 records, duly bound, calendared* and repaired, were delivered to the Corporation at a considerably smaller outlay than the sum of £180 which has just recently been expended upon the four Town Charters and the 119 records of the Guild.

It is only two or three years ago that the Royal Historical Commission deputed Mr. Cordy Jeaffreson, one of the ablest paleographers in the employ of the Government, to inspect the records of Stratford, and the excellence of their then condition is specially alluded to in

---

* It has been publicly stated on several occasions that Mr. Hardy's descriptions *complete* my calendar, words that practically accuse me of negligence; but that gentleman's work is of quite a different character. It is an admirably-executed descriptive analysis of unbound records that I had *previously* calendared.

his Report to the Commission. Having also myself, in the course of my researches, personally examined the ancient records of more than seventy corporate towns in England and Wales, it may not be thought either irrelevant or presumptuous if I venture to express my conviction that the Stratford records, previously to recent operations, were in at least as good a condition as those in any of the towns referred to, and that condition is, in not a few instances, practically unexceptionable.

There is only one piece of neglect of which I have been really guilty. I certainly did forget to mark the unbound records with the numbers given to them in the Calendar, but the inconvenience (if any) that has been created by this oversight must have been very inconsiderable. If any number of persons had wanted to consult the unbound records, the Town Clerk would infallibly have called my attention to the subject, and the defect would have been at once remedied. The identification of records, after a calendar has once been made, is one of the easiest of paleographical tasks, and there could have been no difficulty whatever in the matter.

It only remains to add that the calendar of the records, which I had made for the use of the Corporation, was printed in 1863, without any expense to them, in a thick folio volume, in which considerably over six thousand records are described at sufficient length for ordinary purposes. And the Stratford Herald has no right to assert that the records have been "permitted to lie in the muniment-room at the Birth-Place unclassified, uncalendared, uncared for;" and that they were in a condition that necessitated their reduction "from their chaotic state to something like order," statements conveying the implication that I had thoroughly deceived the Corporation, and involving me in the somewhat humiliating necessity of placing upon record a history of my own labours. Perhaps, however, the Stratford Herald is to be commiserated rather than blamed, if, as is of course possible, it has either been made the victim of a foolish hoax, or if, to make use of the elegant language it has addressed to myself, "its mind has received a particular bias from people whose mental condition renders them incapable of imparting to it the truth."

STRATFORD AMENITIES.

If the Stratford Herald, in mentioning this subject, had restricted itself to observing that the Corporation, *as a body*, have always treated me with "the greatest courtesy," no one would have been justified in disputing the assertion. I have ever felt grateful to them for the kindness with which they have treated me *in their collective capacity*, for the consideration with which they have invariably received the perhaps somewhat too numerous suggestions and requests that I have ventured to make, as well as for the very friendly terms in which they have always expressed the several resolutions that they have been generously desirous of passing in my favour. But when the Herald proceeds to observe, from its "own knowledge," that I have been "treated with the greatest courtesy by every individual member" of the Corporation, it has forgotten for the moment certain speeches that have been reported in its own columns.— The story shall be told as briefly as possible.

In the Spring of last year I offered to be at the risk of producing autotypes of a large

c

number of the Shakespearean town records, the
loss (if any) on the publication to be borne by
myself, the profit (if any) to be handed over to
the Corporation. The spirit in which this proposal was received will be gathered from the
following extract from a report of the proceedings that took place at the meeting at which
my offer was formally accepted.

THE MAYOR said that Mr. Phillipps had undertaken
to supply autotypes at his own risk, and he (the Mayor)
thought the offer a generous one, and ought in some way to
be entertained by the Council. He wanted the opinion of
the Council on the subject.

ALDERMAN COX,—It has reference to the records of
the Council?

THE MAYOR,—Yes.

MR. HODGSON,*—Which are kept in the Shakespeare
Museum?

THE MAYOR,—Yes.

ALDERMAN BIRD thought it was a very desirable thing
to do; but he should disagree with the Corporation taking
the risk. The public would be vastly benefited by the
publication.

THE MAYOR considered Mr. Phillipps's offer very liberal
indeed. (Hear, hear.)

MR. HODGSON,—These valuable documents would go
out of our possession, I presume, into the custody of Mr.
Phillipps.

THE MAYOR,—Necessarily.

MR. HODGSON said that before they did lend them, if
the Council were of opinion that they should comply with
the latter part of Mr. Phillipps's letter—and he hoped the
Council would do so, for he thought it a very nice one—

* Now Sir Arthur Hodgson, K.C.M.G.

every care should be taken that the documents should be carefully numbered and registered.—*Report of the Council Meeting, as given in the Stratford-on-Avon Chronicle, 9 March, 1883.*

Now, it will surely be conceded that, after this, I should have been fully justified in requesting the town-clerk,—and that the town-clerk would have been equally justified in consenting, —to send me to my own residence any documents that were intended to be autotyped, he of course keeping a register of every one so forwarded. Not caring, however, to incur this responsibility, I went a few months afterwards to Stratford to ascertain if the autotyping could not be done on the spot. It fortunately happened that there was an experienced autotyper in the town itself, and it unfortunately happened that the record-room was so narrow and so badly lighted that the accurate reproduction in it of a single document was an utter impossibility. Under these circumstances I took one document at a time (fourteen in all) to the artist's studio, a few hundred yards off, taking care to see that it was at once protected between sheets of plate-glass, and, as soon as it was photographed, returning it myself to its place in the record-room before I took out another. By pursuing this method there was never more than one document absent at a time from the

C 2

record-room, and that under circumstances which precluded the possibility of its being injured.

It is almost incredible, but it is nevertheless a fact, that this harmless and beneficially-intended action of mine was invested by Mr. Charles Flower, one of the most active members of the Corporation, with the dignity of a high crime and misdemeanour. Even if I had been a stranger in the town, yet, having the sanction of the Mayor (see p. 34)—a sanction taken for granted by the Town Council—to the personal loan of the above-mentioned records, and acting, be it ever remembered, in the interests of the Corporation, not in those of my own, it would not have been a graceful act on the part of a member of that Corporation to have instituted a complaint respecting what was at most a technical irregularity in the very limited step that had been taken. Believing myself, however, to have been the accredited literary servant of the Corporation, I can scarcely describe the more than amazement with which I shortly afterwards received the intelligence, from two of the county newspapers, that a censure had been publicly uttered against my mode of procedure.

The circumstances that had surrounded my dealings with the records made this attack upon

me peculiarly singular and ungracious. When
the Corporation accepted my offer in 1862 to
make a calendar of them, I was necessarily invested with an exceptional trust, and was as
much responsible for their safety and preservation as the town-clerk or any other official.
Not only this, but so far from the Corporation
having objected to the temporary removal of a
document from one part of the town to another,
while I was preparing the calendar, and with
the full sanction of everybody, I repeatedly took
one or other over to Mr. W. O. Hunt's house,
and sometimes to Mr. Wheler's, their local
topographical knowledge often enabling me to
complete a description when otherwise I should
have been at fault. I remained in this kind of
quasi-official position for over twenty years, not
one of the three town-clerks who have held
office during that period withdrawing the once
generally appreciated confidence merely because
its bestowal was no longer of much importance
to the town in a commercial point of view.
The result was that, during the whole of that
period, and until Mr. Charles Flower suddenly
commenced to take so absorbing an interest
in the records, whenever I visited Stratford,
efficient study being out of the question in the
dim light of the record-room, I have always felt

myself at liberty to take a volume of documents either into the Museum, or, by their unvarying kind permission, into the residence of the custodians. But here again I was not collecting for the few pages of extracts that were subsequently introduced into the "Outlines," but for references likely to elucidate the history of one or other of the Museum documents. While thus engaged I have been favoured with occasional visits by members of the Corporation, not one of whom ever dropped the remotest hint that I was exceeding my legitimate prerogatives. It has been oddly enough suggested that if these privileges are conceded to me, an inconvenience might arise from the Corporation being expected to grant the same powers to every one else. Assuredly they might be, but only to the every one else who had arranged and calendared their records for them. And, anyhow, if new regulations had been thought to have been advisable, they might surely have been enacted without a public complaint being made against me for having worked under the old ones.

THE "GREATEST COURTESY" SPEECH.

When I replied to the adverse criticism to which I had been subjected, it was generally considered that I did so with too much animation, and that I allowed irritation to "out-run the pauser reason." But it appeared to me from the very first that an objection to the propriety of my action, under the unique position I held in respect to the records, no matter in what or in how mild terms that objection was raised, practically conveyed a slur upon my conduct; and that I correctly appreciated the intentional significance of the original attack will be obvious from the following remarks which Mr. Charles Flower afterwards made in a speech delivered before the Town Council,—

Mr. Halliwell-Phillipps had drawn very largely on his imagination, and possibly his conscience might have told him that *irregular* was the mildest term that could have been applied to those proceedings. He was not aware—he did not think any member of that Council was aware—before reading that pamphlet, that fourteen most valuable documents had been removed from the record-room without the knowledge of the Mayor, or any member of the Corporation, or even of the Town Clerk. He thought a stronger word than *irregular* might be applied to those proceedings.

If the Stratford-on-Avon Herald considers that this language is that of "the greatest courtesy," that journal must belong to a new and advanced ethical school that would exclude so old-fashioned a person as myself from a seat upon its polished benches.

It is clearly insinuated in the above speech that I had not acted in a straightforward manner, and that "my conscience" was most probably aware of that interesting fact; but it is easy enough to see on reflection that the speech is rendered innocuous by its palpable animosity. Its worst feature, as it now appears to me, is that it entirely ignores my long and friendly connexion with the town, as well as that which ought to have been known, after a lengthened experience, not only "to the Corporation but to every individual member of it,"—the impossibility of any action of mine respecting their records not having been taken in what I believed to have been the truest interests of the Shakespearean student and of those of the people of Stratford.

A CONTRAST.

Subsequent proceedings showed unmistakably that the attack made upon me was wholly of a gratuitous character, and that it was not the outcome of a preternatural anxiety for the safety of the records.

Shortly after the delivery of the speech last quoted, Mr. Charles Flower, as chairman of the Record Committee, practically controlled the management of the records, and one of his very first acts was to sanction the transmission of 119 of them to London! There would have been nothing singular in any one else confiding the documents to the perfectly safe custody of the national Record Office, but it is curious that a gentleman who had taken alarm at the risk incurred by my diminutive proceedings should have unhesitatingly encountered another which, however small, was obviously a greater one. If it was proper to incur the latter risk, it follows that Mr. Charles Flower, who had never worked at the records at all, was perfectly right in sending 119 of them over a hundred miles away to be absent for months, while I, who had fagged at them for years, was perfectly wrong in moving 14 a few hundred yards, not a single one of that 14 being permitted to be away from its domicile for more than two or three hours.

The nature of the escort under which the 119 records were conveyed to the metropolis has not transpired. Perhaps Mr. Charles Flower, emulating my care, took one at a time to London, returning it to its place at Stratford before he undertook the responsibility of carrying another. Even in that case he would have submitted them to a greater risk than I did, while the "conscience" of each of us remains, I presume, similarly affected.

OLIGARCHAL ENTHUSIASM.

Bad has begun, but worse remains behind. And a very curious worse it is. Please to recollect the vivid and absorbing interest taken by Mr. Charles Flower and his colleagues in the ancient records of Stratford-on-Avon.

In November, 1886, the Severne collection of documents was sold by public auction, including amongst them the following lots that were thus described in the sale-catalogue :—

221. Confirmation by Robert de Clopton, Knt. to Henry de la Le and Eliz his wife, of a grant by William de Wilmacote, of lands in Clopton. Witn. dom. Peter de Wlnardintone, Robert de Val, William de Sotriche, &c. temp. Hen. III.

222. Grant by Peter de Monteforti, to James de Clopton, of the manor of Clopton, *cum grava*, rent, 10*s*. Witn. dom. William de Bissopesdone, Richard de Wroxhulle, John de Curli, &c. temp. Hen. III.

223. Grants for £40, from James Clopton to Walter de Cokefeld, *dictus marescallus*, and Iohanna, his wife, of his capital messuage and lands in Clopton and in la Graue. Excepting a messuage held by mag. William de Monteforti, parson of Stratford. Witn. dom. John de Wilmecote, dom. William de Bisopisdone, dom. Peter de Woluardintone, &c. temp. Hen. III, seals.—*Five documents*.

225. Grant by Walter de Kokefeld, *dictus marescallus*, lord of Clopton, to James de Clopton, of lands in Schotredesmede and Bischopesdon. Witn. dom. Robart de Val, William Purcel, Philip de Hulle, &c. temp. Hen. III.

226. Grant, for £60, from Peter de Monteforti to Isabel, dau. of Stephen Norton, *clericus*, and Eadmund de Middeltone, her son, of a messuage and lands within the manor of Clopton (tenants and boundaries given). Witn. dom. William de Bisopesdone, Richard de Wroxhul, John de Curli, &c. temp. Hen. III, *seal of arms.*

227. Grants from Isabella de Norton, dau. of Stephen, *dictus clericus*, of Norton, to Walter de Cokefeld, *dictus marescallus*, of the lands acquired from Peter de Monteforti, in Clopton, and Clopton Grove, in Stratford-upon-Avon. Witn. dom. Eadmund de Hegham, dom. Osberd de Berforde, dom. William de Bishopesdone, &c. 8 Edw. I, seals.—*Six documents.*

229. Lease from John, son and heir of James de Clopton, to Walter de Cokefeld or Cokefeud, lord of Clopton, for 100s. of a virgate of land in Clopton and Clopton Grove. Witn. dom. Robert de Val, Knt. William Purcel, Roger de Wotton, *clericus, &c.* Attached is a similar lease, with the addition of a messuage called Ankerhus, in Stratford. Witn. dom. John de Clintone, Knt. Nicholas de Warewyc, Henry de Stratford, fil, Henry de Stowe, &c. 27 Edw. I, seals.— *Three deeds.*

230. Grant by John le barbur, of Stratford, and Margery, his wife, to John Coldelle, of a virgate of land in Clopton. Witn. Henry de Stodleye, Hugh de Chutone, Alan de Schottrethe, &c. 27 Edw. I, *seals.*

231. Lease from John Coldelle to Walter de Cokefelde, lord of Clopton, of land in Clopton. Witn. William Moryn of Snytenfeld, Henry de Hattone, John de Peyto, &c. 32 Edw. I, *seal.*

232. Grant by Robert de Stratford to Walter de Clopton, of a messuage, &c. in Clopton and Grave, and land in Shotryche. Witn. William Saucer, John Gegelyn, William de Utlycote, &c. 3 Edw. III.

233. Exchange by Robert de Stretford, bishop of Chichester, with Walter de Cokefeld, of Clopton, of a place of land called "la Mote," in Clopton, for a meadow in Shotrich. Witn. mag. Henry de Cokham, Adam de Stiuynton, William de Chiltenham, &c. 11 Edw. III, seal.—*Two documents.*

234. Lease from *mag.* John Geronde, *clericus*, formerly rector of Stratford-upon-Avon, to Walter Cokefield and Matilda, his wife, of a place of land in Clopton, next ·Stratford, called "la Mote." Witn. Henry Myle, Adam de Styuentone, Nicholas de Shotryd, &c. 12 Edw. III, *seal.*

235. Lease from John James, of Stratford-upon-Avon, to dom. Robert de Stretford, bishop of Chichester, and Walter de Cokefeld, and Matilda, his wife, of the Manor of Clopton and "in la Grove," and lands in Shotred. Witn. dom. William de Lucy, John Stretham, Knts., John de Peyto, &c. 16 Edw. III, *seal.*

237. Enfeoffment by William, son and heir of John Ermeger, of Stratford, to John Glemham and Rose, his wife, of lands in Stratford, Glemham, Cranysford, Tunstall, &c. 2 Hen. IV, *fine seal of arms.*

238. Copies of five Deeds, as follows: 1. Grant by Richard at Halle and Hugh at Halle, of Stratford-upon-Avon, to Henry Tryg and Johanna, his wife, of lands in Stratford, Aluestone and Tydyngton. Witn. John Iremonger, chief bailiff, John Chebbesey, sub-bailiff, &c. 11 Hen. IV.—Grant by Johanna Brown, of Dymnoke, widow of Henry Tryg or Trigge, to William Rokesley, of Stratford-upon-Avon, of a burgage, &c. there, in Cornestret, and lands in Tedynton (boundaries given) 8 Hen. V.—Release from Thomas Tryg, son and heir of Henry and Johanna, of same to same Power of Attorney and Bond, paper roll.—*Five documents.*

239. Grant by Thomas Mayell, of Stratford-upon-Avon, draper, to John Greswolde, John Mayell and Thomas Leeke, of the same, of all lands held by them in Co. Warwick. Witn. Richard Halle, Thomas Chacombe, bailiff of Stratford, &c., 15 Hen. VI.

240. Grant by Richard Felde, of Kynges Norton, Co. Worc., to Thomas Wouour *als*. Balshale, of Stratford-upon-Avon, of a burgage and croft in Stratford, in Grenehulstrete. Witn. John de Harrapp, and William Staffordshire, sub-bailiffs of Stratford, &c. 24 Hen. VI.

244. Grant by Johanna Iremonger, of Alcettur, widow, to John Clopton, of Stratford-upon-Avon, and Johanna, his wife, of lands in Stratford, in Rotherstreete, called Colyers. Witn. Thomas Clopton, esq., Roger Pagett, Richard Stobbe, Thomas Couper, sub-bailiffs, &c. 19 Edw. IV.

255. Exemplification of a Recovery by John Ichener and William Perrott, from John Clopton of Clopsyll, gent., of 2 messuages, 2 gardens, 2 orchards, and 6 acres of pasture, in Stratford-upon-Avon. 3 Eliz.—*fragment of seal of Queen's Bench.*

256. Lease, for 21 years, from William Clopton, esq., to William Smythe, of Stratford, haberdasher, of a leasowe or pasture in Clopton. Rent 2 capons. 4 Eliz.

261. Lease, for 30 years, by Lodowick Grevell, esq., to Richard Harrington, of Stratford-upon-Avon, yeom., of a messuage and lands in Stratford, and in he ldp. of Ryen Clifford and Bridgtown (described). Rent, £16. 13. 4. 7 Eliz.

267. Grant by William Clopton, esq., to Raffe Sheldon, of Beoley, co. Worc. of lands in Clopton, Reyen Clifford, Bishopstone, &c. for a jointure to Anne his wife, with reversion. 13 Eliz.

269. Lease, for 21 years, by William Clopton, esq., to Peter Smarte, of Stratford-upon-Avon, husbandman, of a close in Clopton. Rent, 26s. 8d. 15 Eliz.

273. Grant for £900, by William Clopton, esq., to John Harvie, of Ickworth, esq., and Henry Griffith, in trust, for George Carewe, esq., and Joyce Clopton his wife, of the Manors of Bridgetown and Ryen Clifford, Co. Warw. 23 Eliz.—*Two documents.*

275. Sale, for £80, by Sir William Catesby, of Ashley Legers, co. Northton, knt., to Thomas Cale, of Bishopton, husbandman, of a messuage and lands in Bishampton, Stratford-upon-Avon, Old Stratford, &c. 24 Eliz.

277. Sale by William Clopton, esq., for £100, to John Skevynton, esq., and John Graye, esq., of the Manor of Clopton, with a messuage, dovecot, &c. in Stratford-upon-Avon. Hilary Term. 24 Eliz.

278. Lease, for 8 years, from the same, to Johanne Sadler, of Stratford, widow, of a windmill in Old Stratford; —rent, a peppercorn. 25 Eliz.

285. Leases, for 11 years, from Sir George Carew, knt., and Joyce, his wife, of the Minories, co. Midd., to Richard Woodward, Thomas Dixon, and Richard Hill, of Stratford-upon-Avon, of lands called Bells Peece, Rye Peece, the Haydon, Arrow Hill, &c. in Bridgetowne. 35 Eliz.—*Four documents.*

286. Sale, for £80, by John Clopton, of Sledwich, co. Durham, esq., to Sir George Carew, knt., Lieut.-Gen. of Ordnance, of the remainder of a lease of lands in Bridgetowne, and Rien Clifford, in par. of Stratford, *same date.*

292. Leases, for 10 years, from Sir George Carew, to John Lane, William Walker and others, of Stratford-upon-Avon, of lands called Crosse, and New Close, Auges, and Harrington's Pikes, Belle's Piece, &c., in Bridgetowne, Ryen Clifforde, and Stratford. 2 Jas. I.—*Six documents.*

294. Lease, for 21 years (with counterpart), from George Lord Carewe, of Clopton, and Joyce his wife, to George Hooker, of London, gent., and William Bristowe, of the Savoye, Midd., of a tenement called the Hermytage, in Bridgetowne. Rent £7. 3 Jas. I.—*Two documents.*

296. Sale, for £40, by William Combe, of Old Stratford, esq., to Simon Cale, of Bishopton, yeom., of 41 "landes" of arable land in Bishopton (described). 9 Jas. I.

297. Grant, to uses, by Symon Cale, of Byshopton, husbandman, to John Fowler, of Worcester, clothier, John Stayte, and others, of messuages and lands in Bushopton, Byshophampton, Stratford, Shottery, &c., in consideration of his marriage with Anne, sister to said John Stayte. 10 Jas. I.

300. Leases from Sir George, Lord Carewe, and Joyce his wife, to John Salisbury, Avery Millard, and Richard

Wright, of lands called Little Rushbrooke, Bridgetowne Farm, Harrington Farm, and Windmill Flat, in Bridgetowne. 17 & 21 Jas. I.—*Three documents.*

304. Leases for 10 years, from Joyce, countess dowager of Totnes, to Francis Ainge, Henry Smith, Avery Millard, and others, of lands called Oxe leasowe, Rammes Close, Great Rushbrooke, and Roxley Heath, in Bridgetown. 9 Ch. I.—*Four documents.*

Now it will be admitted that this collection of documents, all relating to Stratford-on-Avon and its immediate neighbourhood, is of singular local interest,—certainly the most curious assemblage of the kind connected with that town that has ever occurred for sale in the course of my very long experience. Four of the deeds were of special value, those relating to Robert de Stratford, some time Bishop of Chichester, the most eminent inhabitant of the borough during any part of the middle-ages.

The sale was well advertised, and the Stratford oligarchy very properly sent their agent to attend the auction, where he was, I believe, the purchaser of a few articles of a value very inferior to those above described. I have not the pleasure of his personal acquaintance, but, from all that I hear, he was certain to have faithfully carried out to the letter the instructions of his chiefs; and upon a very inexplicable system must those instructions have been based. Strange and almost incredible as it may appear, they sufficed to enable me to purchase the whole of the above-named sixty-six records for the sum of four pounds eight shillings, being exactly at the rate of sixteen-pence each. The four documents of the fourteenth century relating to Robert de Stratford were honoured with a higher estimate, and for those I had to pay the exorbitant sums of one shilling and six-pence a-piece.

The reader will kindly bear in mind the excessive degree of interest taken by the Stratford oligarchy in its ancient records, an interest so devoted and indefinite that it is no wonder they were dissatisfied with what they considered to be my imperfect descriptions of them. It seems that (taking the average) I rarely devoted more than half a dozen lines to the notice of a single document, a very inadequate space indeed for the description of a patrician representative of sixteen-pence sterling.

NOTE.

At the same auction I had the good fortune to acquire the Clopton Cartulary, an ancient folio manuscript volume with its original vellum cover and leather fastenings, that is to say, in precisely the same state in which it appeared as the reference estate-book ages and ages ago at Clopton House. It is the most complete record of that mansion and the adjoining land that is known to exist, but I should hardly have cared to have added it to the Shakespearean collection at Hollingbury Copse had it not included the earliest notice of the poet's estate at New Place that has yet been discovered.

THE HERALD'S EXPLANATIONS.

The preceding pages contain a reprint (with a few corrections and additions) of a little tract in the form in which it originally appeared. These additional notes are elicited by another article in the Stratford Herald, in the course of which appear the following observations,—

A few words may be said respecting Mr. Halliwell-Phillipps's earlier labours in connection with the Corporation documents. *These, it must be admitted, have been considerable, but they seem to have ended when the records of Shakespearean interest were exhausted.* Mr. Halliwell-Phillipps has the frankness to confess that the work was undertaken in "Shakespearean interests and those of his own taste." Engaged in the task to which Mr. Halliwell-Phillipps has devoted the greater portion of his life, one can form some idea of what to him would be the value of the documents in the possession of the Corporation. *Without access to them would he have been able to compile those copious "Outlines" and voluminous "Notes" which are read with so much interest not only by Shakespearean scholars, but by every student of the immortal poet?* If people were so mercenary as to look upon these matters from a business point of view, they might be disposed to assert that Mr. Halliwell-Phillipps had received a *quid pro quo* for his labours. We will not do him the injustice which his champions in the Press are trying to inflict upon a fellow-townsman. We will believe that he engaged in the work, having the highest objects in view, and the real interests of

D 2

the town at heart. Too great a latitude has been given to our remarks, which should only have been applied to those records which did not particularly interest Mr. Halliwell-Phillipps—that were, in fact, in his opinion, of no Shakespearean value. Having used expressions which implied more than we were justified in assuming, we tender to Mr. Halliwell-Phillipps, in all sincerity, our humble apologies. *But may it not be assumed that the records which he deemed of no importance were of the highest value to the Corporation, and, therefore, to the town ? If these were found to be decaying and in a chaotic state, was it not the duty of some one who was cognisant of their value to see that this decay was arrested and the documents duly calendared ?*

It would have given me much pleasure to have accepted these "humble apologies" if their effect had not been neutralized by the passages here italicized—passages which are all founded on erroneous information, and which in a new form repeat the implications that were originally challenged, and are evidently meant to convey the impression that I not only made an important offer to the Corporation solely in my own interests, but that I neglected to carry out effectively the terms of my offer in all directions in which those interests were not affected. The three passages alluded to will now be separately considered.

1. *These, it must be admitted, &c.*—The notion that my labours "seem to have ended when the records of Shakespearean interest were exhausted" is not borne out by the

facts. If this had been the case, my task would indeed have been an easy one. The Corporation records include only twelve documents in which the great dramatist himself is mentioned. In addition to these, there are one containing a notice of his mother, four that mention his uncle Henry, and two referring to his grandfather Richard. Then there are twenty-nine separate documents that include notices of his father, John Shakespeare, who is also frequently mentioned in entries, mostly very brief ones, in the Chamberlains' Accounts, in the Council Books, and in the proceedings of the Court of Record. Out of the more than six thousand records belonging to the Corporation the above make the sum-total of those that relate to the poet and his family, and, if the Calendar had been restricted to the latter, a small pamphlet instead of a thick folio volume would have sufficed for their description.

2. *Without access to them, &c.*—The Herald is under a delusion in thinking that a large number of extracts in my Outlines of the Life of Shakespeare have been derived from the Corporation records. A careful examination of the last edition will show that, exclusive of documents that were printed long before I was

born, *the aggregate of extracts from those records would make only about nine pages of that work !* Much of what little there is of Shakespearean interest in the Stratford records is of the highest value, but most of the materials for the biography are preserved in other collections.

3. *But may it not, &c.*—Here is a reiteration of notions that it was hoped had been satisfactorily disposed of. There was no accruing decay to arrest, as has been already explained at pp. 21, 26 and 28. The utmost that can be said is that a small proportion of the unbound records would have been the better for repairs if expense had been no object, but I can only be fairly censured in the matter for having been too sparing of the Corporation money. The suggestion that I have omitted to calendar records "of the highest importance to the Corporation" is entirely without foundation. *With the exception of some half-dozen documents that have been added to the Record-Room since the Calendar was printed, I have therein described every ancient document in the possession of the Corporation, however small may have been its value in my own estimation.* Under this system over eight hundred miscellaneous records of the Guild have been "duly calendared," although numbers of them are useless indentures refer-

ring to properties that are now impossible of identification, while scarcely any of them bear even in a remote degree on my own studies.

So much for the attempts to convey the notion that I failed in my duty to the Corporation. A few words may now be added respecting the explanation which is given of the singular language quoted at p. 18, but which is really no explanation at all. It appears that one or more persons have been amusing themselves by forwarding to the Stratford Herald, and even "going to the expense of setting-up in type" paragraphs that have been displeasing to that sensitive journal. Its statements of last week were the earliest intimations I had that any paragraphs had been sent to the Herald, or that any one had incurred printing expenses in the matter.* And how in the world their transmission could under any circumstances have been expected to have influenced me is beyond ordinary powers of conjecture.

The Herald concludes its leader with words which appear to imply that I have suppressed

---

* Perhaps I ought to except a long article, entitled *An Ungrateful Town*, criticizing very severely the Corporation and Mr. Charles Flower, which was shown to me in type by the editor of the journal for which it was intended, and which, at my urgent entreaty, was suppressed. But this is the only exception, and it hardly comes within the statement made by the Herald. As to the personalities so justly censured by the Herald, I need scarcely observe that they were as distasteful to me as ever they could have been to Mr. Charles Flower or to any of his friends.

a letter of importance in the fair consideration of the speech quoted at pp. 39, 40. This is not the case. Immediately following the receipt of the letter referred to, before any sort of legitimate time allowed for a reply had expired, and without the excuse of intervening provocation, *another* "greatest courtesy" speech against me had been delivered. One fails to understand how a courteous letter, received under such circumstances, can justify the subsequent delivery of speeches of an opposite description.

In conclusion, let me add that I had hoped, as any one else would reasonably have done under the circumstances, that the letter I addressed to the Corporation in January, 1884,— see a copy of it at p. 71,—one which was most conciliatory in its tone and ordered to be entered on their minutes, would have closed all matters of dispute. So far from this being the case, Mr. Charles Flower, who had seconded the complimentary resolution (p. 70) in my favour, positively initiated almost immediately afterwards another movement against me. It is true that the latter was connected with an institution which was outside the direct influence of the Corporation, but, in a town like Stratford, where the most active leaders belong to both societies, even if there had been no more weighty obstacle, anything like the resumption of pleasant work was obviously impossible. It would, indeed, have been impossible, even previously, had I not consented, by the letter just mentioned, to pass over, for the sake of that work and of peace, the singularly indefensible and more than uncourteous onslaught that had been made upon me for taking the documents to the photographers. But it was now abundantly clear that the denunciatory spirit which had led to the latter inexcusable aggression was only transiently suspended, and that, if I had been weak enough to have made further concessions, I should always have been liable to similar inflictions.

Most people will be of opinion that I should, in justice to myself, have retired upon the occasion of the observations that were made respecting the photographs, a step that I should most assuredly have taken had I been either working for myself or receiving payment for my services. But it must be recollected that my own Stratford researches had practically terminated many years previously, that I was labouring gratuitously, in part under an engagement, in the sole interests of the town, and that it would have been ungenerous on my part to have withdrawn until I had exhausted all possible means for the restoration of harmony. Those means were exhausted when Mr. Charles Flower thought proper to continue the personal altercation, he being then, as now, the chairman of the very committee with whom the Corporation by a specific resolution had desired me to act, my consent to work under that committee, in variation of the terms of my original offer and in opposition to my own predilections, having been moreover solely conceded in deference to their express wishes. Mr. Charles Flower must, indeed, have acquired a singularly exaggerated notion of my poverty of spirit if he

Dost think, I am so muddy, so unsettled,
To appoint myself in this vexation ;

or that it was possible for me to have so completely surrendered every vestige of a decorous consistency as to have attempted to have worked amicably with him in his capacity as the chairman of one committee at the very same time that he was the leader of the hostile opposition to me in his capacity as the chairman of another. It is fortunately not my province to elucidate the theory under which it was thought that a commutative action could have been rationally defended.

THE "MELANCHOLY EVIDENCE."

A republication of the following independent article, and subsequent correspondence, is
necessary in elucidation of more than one
incident of the controversy.

I.—*Copy of an editorial article which appeared in the
Birmingham Daily Post on February the 7th, 1885.*

Mr. J. O. Halliwell-Phillipps—the learned and laborious
Shakespearean scholar—has just issued a second edition
of his recent pamphlet in answer to some charges more
or less vague made against him, and amounting not merely
to omissions, but even to neglect. His pamphlet will
interest all who take any pride in Shakespeare or Stratford,
for the poet and the town owe him an endless debt of
gratitude for the years of labour he has given to the collection of every fragment which can help the modern student
to fill up the scanty sketches of Shakespeare's personal life
and the history of his literary works. Nearly forty years
ago Mr. Halliwell-Phillipps began his researches among the
Stratford records. He found Chaos—he left Kosmos. He
personally examined some 5,823 documents—all in fair
condition—but requiring careful examination and description. Nearly 5,000 of these were afterwards arranged and
bound in twenty-nine volumes, so that now any one of them
can be found in a few minutes when required. A large
folio volume of nearly 500 pages, of which only seventy-
five copies were printed, and which is now worth seven or
eight guineas, was compiled by Mr. Halliwell-Phillipps, as a
" Calendar of the Stratford Records." The whole cost of this
valuable volume was paid by Mr. Halliwell-Phillipps himself,

and many copies were given by him to officials and others in Stratford. So much for what Mr. Halliwell-Phillipps did. Now for what he did not do. The uncalendared documents, numbering 954, consisted of town charters, expired and surrendered leases, miscellaneous documents, and the unbound records of the guild. The late Mr. Wm. Oakes Hunt concurred with Mr. Halliwell-Phillipps in not risking the town charters to the "tender mercies" of the binder's knife, that the miscellaneous documents were of no value entitling them to be bound, and that the 719 expired or surrendered leases were worth keeping, but no more. All the most interesting of these were described in the Calendar (pp. 118–166), and as binding them would have cost £200, it was deemed not worth that sum. The unbound records of the guild did not seem to Mr. Halliwell-Phillipps to be sufficiently original and important to be bound, and he "did not feel authorised to put the Corporation to the expense of having them bound," but about one-half of these have recently been bound, at a cost of £180, of which £64 has been paid by the Corporation, and the balance by the Chairman of the Record Committee (Mr. C. E. Flower). Mr. Halliwell-Phillipps is glad to find that so much money has so readily been found, but enters his "protest against the insinuation that his shortcomings have rendered the outlay a matter of necessity." He further denies that when he finished his work in 1862–63 he left any documents in "a dangerous or perishing condition," and contends that he was not justified in spending public money for what was not prudently necessary; the result was that the cost of the repairs, calendaring, and binding of 4,869 records was less than has recently been paid for a similar treatment of four town Charters and 119 records of the guild. Few, if any, antiquarians and palæographers of our day, even professional experts, could have done so much good work, and have done it so well, as well as so generously; and Mr. Halliwell-Phillipps was entitled to expect a continuation of the freedom of access and courteous help which his great services had so long received. On the occasion of the recent proposal to have autotype *fac-similes* of the most important documents, some friction created much warmth. Some errors and delays led to misunderstandings and the result seems to be that Mr. Halliwell-Phillipps's long literary connection with Stratford-on-Avon is now closed. It is sad to find, and the world generally will find it difficult to believe, that such an ending is possible after forty years of untiring and unselfish work for the literature of the world. In this second edition he gives a complete and apparently unanswerable answer to the kind of charges made more or less directly, and the literary world will remember that it owes Shakespeare's Birthplace and New Place, not to mention a library of Shakespearean books, to the labours of Mr. Halliwell-Phillipps's life.

II.—Copy of a letter which appeared in the same newspaper on February the 7th, 1885, entitled, "The Ancient Indulgences at Stratford-on-Avon."

To the EDITOR *of the* DAILY POST.

SIR,—The Solomons of Stratford on the Record Committee* seem to have made some "remarkable discoveries," something like that of the watch which was found before it had been lost. Fortunately, these are discoveries of "indulgences" some five hundred years old, but the Record Committee will soon want some "indulgences" of a much later date. No doubt all the members of the Record Committee can read the crabbed old manuscripts of five centuries ago, can fill up all the numerous abbreviations, and can translate at sight mediæval ecclesiastical Latin, but

* It appears that there is great indignation in certain local quarters at this body having become a subject for ridicule, but who in the world can help laughing at a Record Committee consisting of gentlemen who are confessedly unable to read a single page of the registers of their own ancient Court of Record? Would not the members of the College of Surgeons be similarly derided if they restricted their anatomical committee to Lord Tennyson and his poetical contemporaries? The constitution of the deliberative body would not be a whit more absurd in one case than in the other. The poets, indeed, would have the best of it, most of them, as is well-known, being versed in the suggestive contents of that very remarkable work, Burton's Anatomy of Melancholy.

they do not seem to have read, or even to have looked at the fac-similes in a folio volume published by one Thomas Fisher some eighty years ago, in which several "Indulgences" found among the Stratford Corporation Records were fully described. They may further be "surprised to hear" that Fisher also gave fac-similes of some indulgences of even older date. I think I remember one or two of 1160 or 1170, and that he gave many pages of careful and valuable fac-similes of documents which the "Record Committee" will probably "discover" in good time with the help of some expert palæographer who, possibly new to the work, may explore and find what Thomas Fisher found in the "summer of 1804," and published in 1807–1809. If the Record Committee will look into Mr. Halliwell's Descriptive Calendar of the Ancient Manuscripts and Records in the possession of the Corporation of Stratford-on-Avon, published in 1863, in a folio volume of nearly 500 pages (viii., 467), they may perhaps be led into the way of further "discoveries," and may possibly find the original MSS. of A Comedy of Errors and Much Ado About Nothing. It is delightful to find that the "ancient indulgences" are to be "framed and glazed" and hung up in the Town Hall, where probably the Town Council, including the Record Commitee, meet. *Vivat Dogberry !*

Your obedient servant,

AN ANCIENT AND MOST QUIET WATCHMAN.

III. Copy of a letter which appeared in the same newspaper on February the 9th, 1885, entitled,—" The Stratford Records and Mr. Halliwell-Phillipps."

To the EDITOR *of the* DAILY POST.

SIR,—I had not intended to say a word respecting the latest melancholy evidence of the spirit which now animates Mr. Halliwell-Phillipps, but when a journal of your importance and circulation in the district, after giving a summary of his work, states that, " in this second edition he gives a complete and apparently unanswerable answer to the kind of charges made more or less directly," it is time that the impression should not be allowed to go abroad that his renewed attacks upon the Corporation of Stratford-on-Avon and myself are unnoticed because they are " unanswerable."

The fact is that all who know the circumstances, or will take the trouble to read Mr. Halliwell-Phillipps's pamphlets, and to refer to the actual reports of the Council meetings, will see what a strange series of mis-statements and perversions of fact he has strung together. His main charge of interference with his freedom of access to the Records seems to be based upon a paragraph taken from a county paper; but he has not the candour to add that he had ascertained before the publication of his first pamphlet that the paragraph gave an erroneous impression of what had taken place. It is indeed "sad to find" that one for whom, up to the issue of these astonishing pamphlets, I had entertained feelings of esteem and regard, should have so wantonly placed himself in a position of hostility to the Corporation, from whom he had received so many favours and such unlimited confidence.

It seems really absurd that Mr. Halliwell-Phillipps should distort into an attack upon himself words which I spoke in reply to charges he had made in about as insulting language as it is possible to imagine, and which charges I proved had not the slightest foundation. I had hoped that, with more leisure to attend to Shakespearean studies, I might have benefited by the advice and assistance he was so well able to give. I can only regret that, as soon as I put my foot upon ground he so well occupied, his friendship should have changed into enmity.

Yours faithfully,

CHARLES E. FLOWER,

Chairman of the Record Committee.

Stratford-on-Avon, February 7, 1885.

IV. Copy of a letter which appeared in the same news-paper on February the 10th, 1885, entitled " The Stratford Records and the Discoveries."

To the EDITOR of the DAILY POST.

SIR,—As there are two sides even to the thinnest slice, so there may be two sides to the question of which the Chairman of the Record Committee gives his own, by imputations of motives to which, doubtless, Mr. Halliwell-Phillipps has a full reply. In the meantime the discoveries are dropped, and no explanation is attempted of the claim to have found what had been found eighty years before. A cloud of controversy is useful when awkward facts are in the way. The facts remain that the Record Committee do not seem to have known what had been done, and to have claimed honours which they did not deserve.

Your obedient servant,

AN ANCIENT AND MOST QUIET WATCHMAN.

V.—Copy of a letter which appeared in the same news-paper on February the 12th, 1885, entitled, " The Stratford Records."

To the EDITOR of the DAILY POST.

SIR,—The letter of Mr. Charles Flower, in your yesterday's paper, deals so vaguely with the only two questions really at issue between the Corporation of Stratford and myself, that you will, I feel sure, kindly allow me to say a few words in elucidation of the subject.

The first question is whether I did or did not neglect my duty in the work on the records that I undertook years ago for the Corporation. It having been lately intimated at Stratford that I did so neglect my duty, I thought it as well to submit to the public a statement of opposing facts which, in the absence of explicit confutation, are clearly " unanswerable." Questions of this kind are not to be decided by mere expressions of opinion on either side, and it is now Mr. Charles Flower's obvious duty to either substantiate his charges of neglect or to withdraw them.

The second question is whether I did or did not commit a breach of privilege in the initial action that I took in the conduct of the autotypes. The Corporation having offered me the personal loan of those records that were to be autotyped, and the record-room being too dark for the operation, it never for a moment occurred to me that I could be doing wrong in taking a few of them, one at a time, to photographers who resided a few hundred yards off. Nor to this day, unless Mr. Charles Flower is entitled, as might appear from his letter, to speak of all Stratford matters in the name of the Corporation, can I believe that any society would be so absurd as to complain of a proceeding taken under the sanction of their own offer. Mr. Charles Flower speaks of my "charge" respecting their "interference with my freedom of access to the records," but so far from making any charge of the kind, I acknowledge with pleasure the courtesy with which they have refrained from such interference during the whole period of my local work of every kind. What interference in such matters, if any may now be, or has lately been, contemplated under the guidance of Mr. Charles Flower, is a contingency that cannot affect me in any way, as I have for some time past definitely relinquished all work on their records.

Mr. Charles Flower is not justified in speaking of my "renewed attacks on the Corporation," unless a temperate defence against injurious surmises broached by certain members of that body can be so interpreted. What I have attacked, and intend, if necessary, to continue to attack, is the gratuitous insolence by which I have been assailed for my harmless and beneficially-intended proceedings in the matter of the autotypes. Mr. Charles Flower accuses me of having published "a strange series of mis-statements and perversions of fact." I challenge him* to prove the

---

* No notice has been taken of this challenge, although it was clearly Mr. Charles Flower's duty to have either withdrawn or substantiated his statement. That he should not have adopted the former course is not very surprising, withdrawals and apologies, excepting as objects of demand, being unknown to the present regime of Stratford-on-Avon.

truth either of this assertion or that of my having made charges against him "in about as insulting language as it is possible to imagine." Mr. Charles Flower then asserts that I had used a paragraph which I had previously ascertained "gave an erroneous impression of what had taken place." It is now some months since I stated my evidences, showing that I had not ascertained anything of the kind. Mr. Charles Flower's reiteration of the charge is, therefore, a wilful aggression.

Should any of your readers desire to learn more on these subjects in greater detail, copies of the third edition of my pamphlet now in the press, will be forwarded, free of expense, to any one sending name and address to

Your obedient servant,
J. O. HALLIWELL-PHILLIPPS.

Hollingbury Copse, Brighton, Feb. 10.

VI.—Copy of a letter which appeared in the same news-paper on February the 13th, 1885, entitled,—" The Stratford Records."

To the EDITOR of the DAILY POST.

SIR,—Conjectural imputations of motives are so outside the bounds of legitimate controversy that I did not, in my yesterday's letter, consider it necessary to reply to Mr. Charles Flower's more than insinuation that I was mean enough to entertain inimical feelings towards him as soon as I found that he was entering upon a course of my favourite studies. As, however, your astute and humorous correspondent, the Ancient and Most Quiet Watchman, appears to think that a disclaimer is called for, I may observe that the view expressed by Mr. Charles Flower is

---

That he could have been successful in an endeavour to verify the above accusation is, I will venture to say, impossible. I may of course have committed oversights in matters of trivial detail, but I have taken the greatest pains to ensure accuracy in every point of the slightest importance, and upon the irrefutable exposition of my case rests my confidence in the nature of the ultimate verdict of public opinion.

one of those arrows which, "too slightly timber'd for so loud a wind," are apt to revert a little way beyond the archer's bow. I have only to remark that my misunderstanding with that gentleman arose a considerable time before he had expressed the slightest intention of troubling himself about the records, and before any sign had appeared that his Shakespearean studies were likely to extend beyond those that had relation to the modern Shakespearean drama cultivated at the Memorial Theatre. My own studies have for many years been restricted to Shakespearean biography and the history of the contemporary stage.

Your obedient servant,

J. O. HALLIWELL-PHILLIPPS.

Hollingbury Copse, Brighton, Feb. 11.

HOSTILITY TO THE COUNCIL.

Now with respect to Mr. Charles Flower's statement of my "having wantonly placed myself in a position of hostility to the Corporation."—For thirty years or more the most cordial and friendly relations existed between that body and myself. It was not until March, 1883, that there was the slightest interruption of harmony. This occurred soon after I had offered to undertake the publication of the Shakespeare autotypes, but the irritation that may have been created on either side by the resulting controversy disappeared under the influences of a conciliatory resolution and an equally conciliatory acknowledgment. The resolution to which I refer was unanimously passed by the Corporation on January the 4th, 1884, in the following terms :—

That this Corporation, fully sensible of the interest taken in their ancient records by Mr. Halliwell-Phillipps, and gratefully acknowledging the important services rendered by him at various times in regard to them, desire to express their regret that he has thought it desirable to abandon the work he had entered upon of autotyping certain of them of special interest; and the Corporation also desire to say further that the confidence they have placed in Mr. Halliwell-Phillipps has never been withdrawn, and they trust that arrangements may be made by the newly-appointed Record Committee which may enable him to resume his valuable labours.

Nothing could possibly be more courteous than the terms of this resolution, but its passage was accompanied by a very singular incident,—it was seconded by Mr. Charles Flower, who, in a speech delivered only a few minutes previously, had attacked me in language of the most seriously aggressive character (see the extract at p. 95). It was natural that I should be perplexed by this odd example of "hot ice and wondrous strange snow," but wishing, if possible, to end all matters amicably, and especially desirous, after receiving so friendly a resolution, that the Corporation should not be subjected to further controversy,—I compelled myself to accept the fact of Mr. Charles Flower's seconding the vote as equivalent to an expression of regret for the violence of his previous speech. Adopting this view, the resolution was acknowledged in the following letter, and the observations made upon it at the Council are here given (from the Stratford Chronicle Report, 8 Feb., 1884), to show how fully it was then considered that all matters in dispute were happily terminated :—

My dear Sir,   Brighton, 19 January, 1884.

I have the pleasure of acknowledging the receipt of copies of the resolutions passed at the last meeting of the Town Council, and I hope that you will take the earliest opportunity of tendering to that body my cordial thanks for the flattering terms in which they have been pleased to speak of my services in respect to the records, and especially for the continued confidence in me so gracefully and unanimously expressed.

I can only say that, so long as I feel that I possess that confidence, and am not subjected to restrictions to which I have been unaccustomed, I shall consider it a privilege to work on the autotypes or in any other way in which my special reading may be useful. It will also give me pleasure to confer with the newly-appointed Record Committee, not merely on the autotypes, but on the general question of the records, and it would be a mere affectation on my part were I not to admit the indulgence of a hope that my very long experience in such matters may enable me to be of service. Believe me, my dear Sir,

Yours faithfully,
J. O. HALLIWELL-PHILLIPPS.

To Thomas Hunt, Esq.,
Town Clerk of Stratford-on-Avon.

The letter was received with loud applause.

COUNCILLOR FLOWER, in moving the adoption of the Record Committee's report, alluded to the pleasure and satisfaction which they would all feel at the receipt of the letter from Mr. Halliwell-Phillipps.

ALDERMAN NEWTON seconded the adoption of the report, and said he was sure they all felt glad that the resolution which was passed at the last meeting of the Council was received in the very best spirit. He also hoped that was the last they would hear of that rather unpleasant episode.

THE MAYOR said that, with regard to Mr. Halliwell-Phillipps's letter, he begged to move "that this most satisfactory letter be placed upon our records."

ALDERMAN COX seconded the motion with the greatest pleasure. He thought it must be exceedingly gratifying to every member of the Corporation to have received that letter, and they might hope that whatever there had been of difficulty or of slight misunderstanding might now be considered to be settled, and that matters with regard to the Record Committee and Mr. Halliwell-Phillipps would now go on smoothly to his satisfaction and to their benefit.

The motion was unanimously adopted.

It was well-known at Stratford that I had a special objection to doing literary work in conjunction with a committee, and the appointment of one was not altogether fair. The conditions under which the services of a gratuitous worker have been accepted should not, in ordinary courtesy, have been materially varied without his consent. It was and is my firm conviction that, while business matters connected with literature may be judiciously left to such a body, literary work itself is always most efficiently conducted by the individual. Waiving, however, this objection, and condoning, for the reasons above stated, the allegations in Mr. Charles Flower's speech,—*that gentleman being then Chairman of the Record Committee,*—I was holding out to him an unconditional olive-branch by working cordially and amicably with that committee. That I did so work will be apparent from the following letter which I addressed to the town-clerk a few weeks afterwards,—

Brighton, 13th February, 1884.

My dear Sir,—

I have the pleasure of returning you Mr. Hardy's report, and would venture to submit the following observations upon it :—

1. With respect to the documents, drawings, engravings, and papers in the custody of the Birth-Place Trustees, instructions were given at the last meeting of those trustees to Dr. Ingleby and myself to see what could best be done towards the formation of a greatly-wanted Calendar of them. It was not easy to find a competent person for such a task, for it requires one who has not only a manuscript and record experience, but also a considerable acquaintance with the literature of the Shakespearean period. After some months' consideration, we decided to recommend as calendarist Mr. G. F. Warner, of the Manuscript Department of the British Museum, and we have ascertained from that gentleman that he is willing to undertake the work. This recommendation is, of course, subject to the approval of the trustees, but it is not likely that Mr. Warner's nomination will be opposed, the Governors of Dulwich College having engaged him a few years ago to make a catalogue of their somewhat cognate collection of ancient deeds and old dramatic manuscripts, the result being a calendar that is acknowledged to be one of the best ever published.

2. With respect to the records of the Corporation— those now under the care of your Committee—they will be most conveniently considered in the two classes of bound and unbound manuscripts.

All the bound manuscripts have been fully calendared, and having been repaired and mounted at the British

Museum by the most experienced manuscript binders in the world, no question can arise as to the necessity for any of these being again sent to London.

The unbound manuscripts form a very small portion of the collection, and if, as is stated, there are any amongst them not to be found in the printed calendar, it must be that some have been discovered and placed in the drawers since that calendar was printed in 1863. I work at these matters so extremely methodically, it is hardly possible that I could otherwise have overlooked any, and especially, according to Mr. Hardy, "a large portion,"—but this latter statement is surely, as will be seen, founded on misapprehension.

Mr. Hardy, in drawing up his report, was evidently not aware that a year or two ago Mr. Cordy Jeaffreson made an examination of your records on behalf of the Historical Manuscript Commission, and in the last Report of that Commission, issued a few days ago, there is printed an elaborate "List of the Unbound Records in the Stratford-on-Avon muniment-room."

It would take time and care to ascertain how many in this list are unmentioned in the printed calendar, but I have already, during the few days that have elapsed since the report was published, identified all but nine as being described in that Calendar. I may, therefore, be pardoned for suspecting that even this very small list of omissions may be still further reduced. It is worth notice that Mr. Cordy Jeaffreson mentions as "the most remarkable of the hitherto unnoticed documents" the Letters of Indulgence of 1270. Now this very document will be found described in my printed Calendar, p. 252, No. 65. It is true that it is only briefly catalogued, but the proper office of a calendarist is merely to say what the documents are, not to enter upon the value or curiosity of each. Had I adopted the latter system, I should have had to print a dozen folio volumes instead of one.

Any of the records are, of course, perfectly safe when they have once reached the Record Office, but there is always a certain amount of risk, however infinitesimal, of danger in transmission. If the committee will kindly excuse the suggestion, it will be best to lay down a rule that no records bearing on the history of Shakespeare or his family should be allowed to go out of the town. Most of the bound volumes include documents that come under this denomination, and the trifling degree of risk previously referred to should not, without urgent necessity, be encountered in respect to muniments of such priceless value.

None of the unbound records include notices of either Shakespeare or his family, and, as many of them seem to require repair, it is hardly necessary to say that, as that special work could not be done at Stratford, no better arrangement could possibly be made for that purpose than sending them to the Public Record Office to the care of so experienced a paleographer as Mr. Hardy.

Begging you to do me the favour of placing this letter before the committee, Believe me,

Yours faithfully,

J. O. HALLIWELL-PHILLIPPS.

To Thomas Hunt, Esq.,
Town-Clerk of Stratford-on-Avon.

Taking it for granted that all things would now continue to go on quite smoothly, my regret may be well imagined when I learnt only two days afterwards that the Chairman of the Record Committee was the leader in an aggressive movement directed against me in the name of the Executive Committee of the Birth-Place. Although this latter controversy was outside the function or notice of the Corporation, I clearly saw that further pleasant work with their Record Committee was out of the question, and at once determined to retire from the scene. It did not, however, appear to be necessary to trouble the Corporation with a formal announcement to that effect, and there was not the semblance of a ground of complaint on my part against the Corporation. So far from this, when they were recently accused of treating me discourteously, I thought it my duty to correct the statement in the following letter which appeared in one of the October numbers of *Truth*,—

Brighton, Oct. 18th, 1884.

Sir,

Will you kindly allow me to say a few words in reference to a paragraph in your last number?

It is true that I have been treated with "scant courtesy" by certain individuals at Stratford-on-Avon, who have made the place a less agreeable workshop to me than heretofore, but I have received nothing but kindness from the main body of the Corporation. During the many years that I have held honorary relations with that Corporation, no request of mine has been refused, nor have I the least reason for suspecting that an exception would now be made. At the same time I have made up my mind to have nothing further to do with the conduct of the Shakespeare autotypes; but this determination is the result of circumstances in which the Corporation, as a body, have had no share.

I am, Sir,

Your obedient Servant,

J. O. HALLIWELL-PHILLIPPS.

To the Editor of Truth.

So much for the accusation that I have made "renewed attacks upon the Corporation of Stratford-on-Avon." Now let us see what grounds there are for Mr. Charles Flower's allusion to the "many favours" that he alleges I have received from that body.

Of "favours" from the Corporation, of any that can be reasonably so called, either few or many, I have received absolutely none. The facilities that I have enjoyed for my Shakespearean researches cannot be regarded in the light of that term, for that would be to imply that the Corporation were not voluntarily anxious to encourage such researches. So far from the latter being the case, they have always shown an enlightened desire to facilitate the work of all students who have come before them with legitimate objects of enquiry. As for other kind of "favours," I have solicited none from the Corporation that have not been demanded in their own interests, while I have ever carefully refrained from asking for—and it was well known that I would not have accepted —a single penny for myself. This was not from a want of reliance on their liberality, for I knew perfectly well that if I had but hinted that I wished my personal expenses to be defrayed, or to have received a donation towards the expense of printing the Calendar, the money would have been immediately and cheerfully voted. But throughout my long connexion with Stratford-on-Avon I have been determined to sustain an absolutely independent position, and have at least been successful in that direction.

Neither can I admit that the "unlimited confidence" awarded me by the Corporation was in any sense whatever a "favour" to myself. It was the necessary result of their acceptance of my offer to calendar their records. In the absence of "unlimited confidence," the preparation of that volume would have been an impossibility. Even with the unrestricted facilities that were afforded, being otherwise intensely occupied, I had to work double tides to manage its preparation. If it had been necessary for me to wait on every occasion for the attendance of the Town Clerk, the waste of time alone would have stifled the whole design, so that my control over the record-keys, when I was at Stratford, was really an essential feature of the contract.

Mr. Charles Flower speaks of my "main charge of interference with my freedom of access to the records." Having some time ago expressed my intention of having nothing further to do with the records, this statement would have been objectless even if it had been correct. But, instead of being correct, it is absolutely devoid of foundation. I have made no charge of the kind, nor had I the slightest grounds for doing so. The Corporation have never either directly or indirectly intimated that they wished to curtail the facilities that were necessary when I was working for them, and had since naturally become habitual privileges. A movement in that direction would have been inconsistent with their vote of confidence, and with their acceptance of the terms of my acknowledgment of that vote. My retirement from the Corporation record-work has no connexion whatever with this subject, but it is entirely owing, as has already been stated, to circumstances over which they have no jurisdiction.

It is Mr. Charles Flower, not I, who has made "charges," and by one of his respecting the autotypes he has intimated that I was not as solicitous as I ought to have been for the safety of the records. This surmise is wholly unjustifiable. I can venture to say that no one could possibly have taken a more affectionate care of them than either the late Mr. W. O. Hunt or myself.

Mr. Hunt very properly laid down a stringent rule that, excepting in those rare cases where substantial reasons could be given for its infringement, no record was to be moved beyond the precincts of Stratford, but he always gave me complete liberty to take a volume of them into any part of the town that I pleased, either for reference, or for light, or for comparison. Was this a "privilege" on my part too extravagant to be enjoyed in my exceptional position of the Corporation's honorary calendarist? If the transmitter of the 119 records to London asserts that the late Mr. W. O. Hunt's ruling in this or any other matter is deserving of condemnation, then I know that there will not be wanting those who will rise in indignation at a slur being so passed upon the memory of the most revered son of modern Stratford,—upon that of one who was for nearly fifty years the ablest and the most devoted servant of its Corporation.

THE CALENDAR OF THE RECORDS.

It is only charitable to assume that the implication conveyed by the surmises of the "many favours" and the "quid pro quo" was not an intentional misrepresentation, but it is none the less offensive or the less inexcusable on that account. Before people indulge in assertions that lead up to derogatory interpretations it is their duty to make themselves acquainted with the facts of the case. The insinuation has been neither more nor less than one to the effect that I was furtively collecting for my own personal objects under the pretence of working in the interests of the Corporation and the town; and it is hardly possible to imagine an imputation that can be further removed from the truth.

Before the spring of 1848 I had gone through all the Stratford records for Shakespeare-biographical purposes, this circumstance being alluded to in the following terms in the Preface to my Life of Shakespeare published in that year,—"in the council-chamber of Stratford-on-Avon are preserved vast quantities

F

of manuscript papers, commencing at a very early period, and particularly rich in materials for a history of that town during the reign of Elizabeth ;—all these I have carefully perused, —attractive bundles filling large boxes, chests, drawers and cupboards,—and the important and novel information thence collected is fully exhibited in the following pages." A few years afterwards I made another minute examination of the town records, *the result being that every Shakespearean document in the possession of the Corporation was printed in the next edition of my work that appeared in 1853, nine years before the Calendar was commenced.*

As I have already observed, exclusively of documents printed before I was born, there are only about nine pages of my " Outlines" taken from the town records. Now if we exclude everything in that work that had been published in or before the year 1853, there are less than two pages of new matter derived from those records, and this in a book of seven hundred and eighty-four pages, those two pages, more-over, consisting of dispersed extracts that are merely illustrative of more important facts derived from other sources. Even these ex-tracts were, I believe, taken in the researches that were made before 1853. Considering that the work of calendaring was not commenced till 1862, there is something more than indefensible in the insinuation, on the part of the present leaders of public opinion in Stratford, that I undertook that very laborious task for the sake of obtaining information in aid of my own publication. What makes the matter far worse is their studied suppression of all allusion to my having printed the Calendar in a thick folio volume at my own expense, a fact that in the minds of all fair-dealing persons would in itself have averted the very possibility of the quid-pro-quo suggestion.

In striking contrast with all this is the gentlemanly reception that my labours met with at the time at the hands of the Corporation, whose appreciation of them was embodied in the following resolution,—

Borough of Stratford-upon-Avon.—At a Quarterly Meeting of the Council held at the Guildhall on Wednesday, the 5th day of August, 1863, Edward Fordham Flower, Esq., Mayor, in the Chair, it was moved by Mr. Alderman Kendall, seconded by Mr. Councillor Bird, and resolved unanimously, that the best thanks of the Council be given to J. O. Halliwell-Phillipps, Esq., for the liberal present of two copies of his Calendar of the Records of this Corporation ; and the Council desire to take this opportunity of expressing the deep sense they entertain of his disinterestedness and zeal in thus giving to the world a descriptive account of their valuable and interesting records, a work of great labour, undertaken without any hope of reward except-

ing the satisfaction arising from the fact that his labours
were exercised upon documents intimately connected with
the birth-place of the great bard, whose genius and writings,
and the history of whose life, Mr. Halliwell-Phillipps has
done so much to elucidate and explain, and to whose
memory he has so effectively directed the minds of the
present generation. The Council desire also to thank Mr.
Halliwell-Phillipps for the interest he has taken in the binding and preservation of the town records, and the valuable
suggestions he has made to that end. That a copy of this
resolution, sealed with the Common Seal, be framed and
glazed, and formally presented to Mr. Halliwell-Phillipps.

The Corporation, indeed, have never been
wanting in the courtesy due to the hardest
gratuitous worker that Stratford has ever possessed, and I feel sure that, if I had filled two
hundred instead of two pages of my "Outlines"
with extracts from their records, it would not
have influenced their estimate of my services.
Instead of attributing selfish motives to me
on that account, they have always, and this is
even implied in some of the terms of the above
resolution, expressed themselves indebted to all
zealous investigators of the details of Shakespearean biography, upon the truthful study of
which really depends the permanence of Stratford's celebrity. They would assuredly have
concurred in the sentiments that were thus
expressed in a letter that the late Mr. W. O.
Hunt addressed to me in 1847,—" my earnest
wish is that every document which will throw

the least light upon the life of the inimitable poet should be published without delay, lest any damage happen to the originals, and for this purpose I will afford every opportunity in my power."

Mr. Hunt's wishes were speedily realised, and the Stratford records, although of eminent value to the local historian, are now practically of none to the Shakespearean biographer, every document that can be of the slightest use to him in his researches having long since been published and as well known to the student as the grave-stone or monumental effigy. It may, indeed, be safely asserted that there is not a single known probable source of record Shakespeare-biographical information in all Warwickshire that has not been exhaustively worked. Accident of course may bring something of value to light from hitherto unmentioned recesses, but how great is the improbability may be gathered from the curious circumstance that the Stratford Herald, a paper which has always followed its obvious duty in encouraging Shakespearean communications during the many years of its existence, has never to this day obtained a single new fact that could be introduced into a reasonable Life of the great dramatist. What has been useful has not been new, and what has been new has not been useful. This is not said in depreciation of that journal, it being obvious that the conductors of a general-information newspaper cannot be expected to have at hand references that are familiar only to specialists of mature experience ; but still it is singular that no one of its correspondents should either have added to our knowledge of the poet's biography, or even have indicated the only large repository of unexhausted materials that is within the easy reach of the local enquirer.

At Worcester will be found a nearly unexplored mine which is all but certain to yield new information of value both to the local historian and to the Shakespearean biographer. I have gone carefully through the corporate records of that city as well as those which are in the Diocesan Registry, but an effective examination of the immense number of wills, inventories, administrations and licenses, which are preserved in the District Registry of the Court of Probate, could not be completed under a continuous labour of several years, and this has all along been beyond my reach. That much is there to be found may be gathered from my having discovered, in a fortnight's search during the present summer, an important document respecting Richard Shakespeare of Snitterfield and his son John, the latter of whom was the poet's father, as well as several incidental notices of both of them and other valuable evidences. Stratford being within an easy drive of that office, which is daily open to the public from 10 to 4 on the payment of moderate fees, surely some of its Shakespearean votaries will be found to continue the work, one that is certain to yield more useful results than the search for imaginary quid-pro-quos and unconferred favours.

EXAMPLES OF THE "FAVOURS."

1. When the estate of New Place was purchased in the year 1861, it was thought desirable, and, indeed, a duty to the subscribers, to place on record the evidences by which its identity and exact boundaries were determined. I spent many laborious months in the prosecution of this task, embodying the results of my enquiries in a large folio volume, copiously illustrated, in which the history and topography of the property were set forth in minute detail, both in their connexion with Stratford-on-Avon and with Shakespearean biography, from the fifteenth century to the time of the purchase. Copies were liberally distributed in the town, none being subscribed for either there or elsewhere, the whole of the expenses being borne by myself. In acknowledgment of the copy presented to the Corporation I had the pleasure of receiving a transcript of the following resolution,—

Borough of Stratford-upon-Avon.—At a Quarterly Meeting of the Council held at the Guildhall on Wednesday, the 7th February, 1866, the Town-Clerk informed the Council that Mr. J. O. Halliwell-Phillipps had transmitted a copy of his History of New Place which he desired to present to the Corporation to be kept in their Record-Room.   Moved by Alderman Kingsley, seconded by Alderman Kendall, and unanimously resolved, that the Council beg to express their best thanks to Mr. Halliwell-Phillipps for the presentation of this valuable and interesting book, and at the same time to acknowledge their high sense of his multifarious acts of liberality and generosity to the Corporation and their appreciation of this additional evidence of the warm interest he takes in everything connected with the history of the borough.

2. In the year 1864 I compiled an account (printed in a folio volume) of the Council Books marked A and B, the work being extremely laborious, owing to the perplexing manner in which a large number of the entries had been originally inserted ; the Corporation, in acknowledging the receipt of their presentation copy, passing the following resolution,—

At a Meeting of the Council of the Borough of Stratford-upon-Avon held at the Guildhall on the 7th day of December, 1864, the Mayor read a letter from J. O. Halliwell-Phillipps, Esq., F.R.S., accompanied by a copy of a new work prepared by him and printed at his own expense containing a minute account of the two earliest Council-Books of this borough, marked A and B, extending from 1563 to 1628, of which he begged the acceptance of the Corporation.   Moved by Alderman Kendall, seconded by Alderman Freer, and resolved unanimously, that the Council accept with great pleasure Mr. Halliwell-Phillipps's interesting and valuable gift, and desire to convey to him their grateful thanks for the excessive care and trouble he has so kindly taken in executing gratuitously the very difficult task of deciphering and rendering legible to all readers the abbreviations and obscure manuscripts contained in these old Council-Books commencing three centuries ago. The Council are pleased to take this opportunity to renew their best acknowledgments to Mr. Halliwell-Phillipps for his liberal presents to the Corporation on former occasions, and for his disinterested exertions to secure for the public every relic calculated to elucidate the domestic life and character of Shakespeare and the history of this his native town. That this resolution be copied on parchment, and sealed with the Common Seal in the presence of the Mayor, and be then framed and glazed and transmitted by the Town-Clerk to Mr. Halliwell-Phillipps.

Let me here mention that, until impelled by recent occurrences, I never dreamt of alluding to any services that I may have rendered the town of Stratford, but there are circumstances under which a little egotism is not only excusable but a necessity in self-defence. As a well-known author lately observed under conditions similar to those in which I am now placed,—"when a man is attacked in the way I have been, he must say something for himself."

THE INTANGIBLE SHAKESPEARE.

When I said that I had described in my Calendar of 1863 every ancient document then in the possession of the Corporation, I ought to have added that one omission might reasonably be inferred from the following statement which appears in a recent number of the English Illustrated Magazine,—

The curious entry relating to him (Shakespeare) in the diary of his cousin, Thomas Greene, clerk of the Corporation of Stratford, has just been autotyped. Thanks to the kindness of the present mayor (Sir Arthur Hodgson) and the town-clerk, we were enabled to see the original document. *We looked on its crooked, almost illegible characters, with no little reverence, as being one of the very few authentic relics of that intangible person, William Shakespeare.* Greene writes from London:—"1614, Jovis 17, No. My cousin Shakspeare coming yesterday to town, I went to see him how he did. He told me that they assured him they meant to inclose no further than to Gospel Bush, and so up straight (leaving out part of the Dingles to the field) to the gate in Clopton hedge, and take in Salisbury's piece; and that they mean in April to survey the land, and then give satisfaction, and not before; and he and Mr. Hall say they think there will be nothing done at all."

It must be admitted that no notice of the document here quoted will be found in my Calendar, but then I have this to say in my defence, viz., *that it is neither in the Record*

Room nor in the possession of the Corporation at all! It was no doubt thought, and perhaps correctly, that one old document was as good as another in a town where neither could be read ; but still it was too cruel of Sir Arthur Hodgson to allow a confiding visitor to go into unnecessary raptures over a visionary relic ; at the same time that he was exposing me to a charge of serious negligence in omitting all notice of what would have been,—if it had only been there!—one of the most interesting records in the collection. The authoress of the charmingly-written paper above quoted, who does not assume to be a paleographical reader, necessarily relied on the exhibit being the real Simon Pure ; little thinking that the latter was preserved in another repository. "Please, sir, will you tell me which is the Duke of Wellington and which is Napoleon Bonaparty," imploringly enquired a little girl of the keeper of a penny peep-show. "Vichever you please, my pretty little dear," replied the accommodating proprietor, "you pays your money and you takes your choice." No wonder that the great dramatist is termed an "intangible person" when a biographical evidence is the object of a similar contempt for accurate identification even in his own native town.

THE "IRREGULAR" ENQUIRY.

Perhaps,—I speak hesitatingly in the midst of so much rough treatment,—but perhaps the most striking example of the ungentlemanly manner in which I have been assailed will be found in the following extract from a speech publicly delivered by Mr. Charles Flower before a meeting of the Town Council,—

To account for the difference in tone of my letter of December 1st and my speech of December 4th, I must explain that the letter was written under the idea that Mr. Halliwell-Phillipps had been acting under an erroneous but honest impression. I even thought it possible that I might have used the word *irregular* at the former meeting, although I had no recollection of having done so. It was only on the evening of December 3rd that I ascertained from the newspapers that had reporters present that I had not used the word at all, and learned *that Mr. Halliwell-Phillipps had himself made enquiries, and knew before he issued his pamphlet that I had not used the word to which he objected.* This, of course, entirely altered the complexion of the case, *and showed that the mis-quotation was made deliberately* instead of, as I had supposed, from some mis-information.

The passages given in italics are utterly false. Not having been at Stratford at the time, and no oral communication having passed between any one connected with the town and myself, it follows that my only sources of information were those that were afforded by epistolary correspondence. Now the only correspondence that I had on the subject of the Council meeting was with the two Stratford newspapers, and in their replies, which are now before me, and which are in answer to my enquiries respecting the completeness of their published reports, there is neither a syllable referring to the word *irregular*, nor an allusion to anything whatever that Mr. Charles Flower was supposed to have uttered. At the same time I held, and still hold, absolute evidence that neither of those published reports contain the whole of what was said on the occasion.

The speech's offence is aggravated by the fact that I had already given a refutation of the calumny when it had been broached by Mr. Charles Flower on a previous occasion. Having, however, condoned the repetition of the insult for the reasons given at p. 70, I could not of course have resuscitated the subject if Mr. Charles Flower himself had not, for the third time, promulgated his deliberate misrepresentation (see p. 63) in a manner that would lead the public to believe that it had never been contradicted.

THE BIRTH-PLACE MUSEUM.

It was observed by Mr. Charles Flower, at the last meeting of the Trustees, held in the May of this year, 1886, speaking of the manuscripts preserved at the Birth-Place, that " Mr. Halliwell-Phillipps had them bound, looking after those only which were of Shakespearean interest, and letting the others go anywhere." If I had done so, I should not have been greatly blamed by my fellow-students,* but in point of fact, having worked throughout my Stratford career with constant reference to the local interests, I paid nearly as much attention to the Stratford as I did to the Shakespearean

---

* However limited may be the value of Shakespearean biography in the opinion of a large number of the critics, to say nothing of its absolute inutility to the odd people who believe Shakespeare to have been somebody else, there can be no doubt of its being everything to Stratford-on-Avon, a town which, in its absence, would be merely one of our Little Pedlingtons. It is, therefore, with infinite amazement that one observes indications, on the part of its present rulers, to place the study of the history of the town on a level with that of the history of the poet. There is an unmistakable evidence of this in the prominence that has been given, during the three opening years of the Record Committee, to the medieval documents, which are in fact the only ones that they have taken in hand, and which are absolutely valueless to the Shakespearean student. It is now announced that Mr. Hardy is to be further engaged on the same series of comparatively worthless documents, an arrangement greatly to be deplored when his skilled services amidst the inexhaustible stores of our national Record Office would be certain to yield information of high value respecting Shakespeare's Stratford, and in all probability new facts of importance respecting the great dramatist himself.

G

documents. The latter forming an infinitesimal portion of the collection, Mr. Charles Flower's words involve an implication of negligence on my part in respect to nearly the whole of the documents, and, under these circumstances, a few words on the system that was followed in my work may not be thought irrelevant.

When the Museum was founded some time about the year 1862, by Mr. W. O. Hunt and myself, our main object was of course to obtain articles of Shakespearean interest, but we included in our design those which were illustrative of the history of Stratford-on-Avon and of some of the adjacent hamlets and villages, including Bishopton, Shottery, Wilmecote and Snitterfield. There was only one point upon which we materially differed. Mr. Hunt was for excluding printed notices of modern date, such as hand-bills, &c., whereas I was in favour of preserving everything that could be obtained, having seen how often the ephemeral productions of one generation become useful to the next. And Mr. Hunt eventually let me have my own way, thus securing for the Museum every sort of record in the town that I could get hold of, from medieval documents to recent announcements of the advent of a wild-beast show.

Proceeding upon this system I persuaded the late Mr. Edward Adams to make up for the Museum a complete set of the Stratford Herald from its commencement. Few articles are more difficult to obtain than old sets of provincial journals, and it is scarcely necessary to say how important they become to the local historian. Of the first Stratford newspaper, published from 1749 to 1753, single copies only of five or six numbers are now known to exist, and I am probably the only person living who has read through a complete file, one, believed to have been unique, having perished with the rest of the Longbridge rarities.

A very considerable number of the early deeds and papers respecting Stratford-on-Avon, Wilmecote and Snitterfield, now in the Museum, were obtained by my own personal exertions, and in this way. Attached to Mr. Hunt's offices was a large room containing many thousands of documents, including, as would naturally be the case with a firm of solicitors that had been established considerably upwards of a century, a vast number that had become legally useless. I minutely explored the contents of this room, a task that occupied many weeks, it being arranged that, whenever I found a document suitable for the Museum, I should submit it to Mr. Hunt, before placing it in that depository, in order that he might be perfectly sure that it neither belonged nor could be of use to any of his clients. In this work I was at intervals materially assisted by my old friend, Mr. Thomas Hunt, the present town-clerk, who, however, made no scruple in expressing his decided opinion that a person who, without a liberal fee, could spend a long summer's day poring over deeds in a musty room instead of taking a fishing excursion, was a palpable lunatic.

Mr. Charles Flower then complains of "the way in which many of the documents at the Birth-Place are mixed up, a valuable parchment deed coming next, perhaps, to a newspaper report of Stratford races."

This defect, if defect it be, is easily explained. The documents came in very gradually during a number of years, and my plan was to have all loose papers bound in volumes as soon as possible after their delivery, a plan that I feel sure was best conducive to their preservation, and to as convenient reference as was possible under the circumstances. One might have waited for half a century before there were accumulated a sufficient number for a volume of "valuable parchment deeds" that were suitable for binding (the seals of most of such relics excluding them from that operation), or for another one of reports on Stratford races. In a collection subject to continual increase,—two hundred documents have, I understand, been presented during the present year,—a definite arrangement is practically impossible, for it would necessitate a rebinding of the whole whenever a parcel of articles of a miscellaneous character were added to the Museum. Few things are easier than to compile a chronological table of contents to a calendar, and in that way all serious inconvenience to the student from the want of a chronological arrangement in the calendar itself would be obviated.

Then Mr. Charles Flower, speaking of the main collections in the Museum, observed that they "were not the gifts of Mr. Halliwell-Phillipps or Mr. Hunt entirely, but simply brought together by them." These words are calculated to convey an erroneous impression.

The gifts of the late Mr. W. O. Hunt were in the aggregate of enormous importance to the town. For the sake of the Museum he stripped his house of nearly every article of Shakespearean interest, including some of the highest rarity and pecuniary value, independently of what is generally termed the Stratford

Portrait, for which alone it is well-known that he received an offer of a thousand pounds. His other gifts included the valuable court-roll of Getley's Copyhold, 1602, one of the few documents now in existence that must have been in the hands of the great dramatist himself. Mr. Hunt, writing to me on August the 24th, 1865, observes,—"you will be pleased to hear that I have this day placed in the Museum, as a gift by me, my beautiful illustrated edition of Shakespeare in twelve vols. 4to, and I assure you it cuts a good figure in the book-case;—this will be the last of my donations, and I prefer giving what I have done in my life-time, as it not only saves the expense of legacy-duty, but trouble to my representatives hereafter;—we have had enough too already of gifts by will in Thomson *v.* Shakespeare;— it is fortunate I prevailed upon Miss Wheler to make her presents at once, for we might have waited for many years and then probably have had a dispute with her executors, besides the annoyance and expense."

It was entirely owing to the incessant entreaties of Mr. Hunt that the invaluable Wheler collection was secured for the town.

My own gifts to the Museum were of far smaller importance than those which were contributed by Mr. Hunt, but they were not altogether insignificant. They included about five hundred volumes of printed Shakespeareana, the early oil painting of Windsor showing the street where Falstaff is said to have been carried down in the buck-basket, and Greene's original drawing of the Jubilee Amphitheatre, 1769, of local interest as the only contemporary sketch of that building known to be preserved.

For many years the Museum was the object of my earnest solicitude. I can safely say that, with very few exceptions indeed, my numerous visits to Stratford-on-Avon from 1864 to 1883 were made all but exclusively in its interests.

On the occasion of my last visit I spent a week, at serious personal inconvenience, solely and entirely in arranging a large parcel of single-leaved manuscripts that had been presented to the Museum by Mr. Bush. It was a task that involved the careful perusal of nearly every document, and unless the Stratford oligarchy are far more obtuse than I take them to be, I must have expended more time over this one piece of business than they do in a year over their annual report on Shakespearean matters. Their labours in that direction for the entire twelvemonth ending in last May, 1887, yielded eighteen printed lines.

Yet these are the gentlemen who had the effrontery to complain of the brevity of some of the descriptions in my Calendar of the Town Records, a laborious compilation consisting of 466 folio pages of close print, each page containing 42 lines. At their rate of work that Calendar would have furnished the Stratford oligarchy with tranquil occupation for over a thousand years.

My Stratford work having terminated, and under circumstances that exclude the possibility of its resumption, if the present magnates of the town, not caring to offer me so much as a thank-you for my long-continued services, prefer to subject them to adverse criticism, one would have thought that the latter might have been conducted with a little more regard to fairness and accuracy of fact.

OPINIONS OF THE PRESS.

His work finished, Mr. Halliwell-Phillipps returned home with the well-earned sense of having done his best, and leaving, as he admits in his pamphlet, but one thing undone, namely, to mark the unbound records with the numbers given to them in the calendar, but, as he justly adds, the "inconvenience (if any) that has been created by this oversight must have been very inconsiderable." It was with the greatest amazement, therefore, that he read the following remarks in a leading article in a recent issue of the Stratford-on-Avon Herald :—" The Stratford Corporation are in possession of many very interesting records extending from the earliest times, but it is only recently that the value of these documents has dawned upon the corporate mind ; —they were permitted to lie in the muniment-room at the Birth-Place unclassified, uncalendared, uncared for, and this indifference to their existence, had it continued, would have led ultimately to their decay and consequent loss to the town." No severer judgment could have been passed upon him, and Mr. Halliwell-Phillipps rises in natural and just indignation to defend himself against the implied charge of gross neglect. The strictures upon him are both unkind and uncalled for.—*The United States Shakespeareana.*

Allusion has more than once been made to the curious and humiliating controversy into which Mr. Halliwell-Phillipps has recently been drawn with certain members of the Council of Stratford-on-Avon. That controversy has just resulted in the most painful of possible issues, for it has ended in the total severance, on the part of the eminent Shakespearean scholar, of all literary connection with the native town of the national dramatist. The course adopted by Mr. Halliwell-Phillipps was the only one at all compatible with the respect that a thorough student and perfect gentleman owes to himself and to his subject. That Mr. Halliwell-Phillipps's friends may feel strongly in this matter of the treatment he has had at the hands of Stratford officials is perhaps a smaller concern, but it is not unimportant where a decision of such consequence is in question. Mr. Halliwell-Phillipps is not a young man fighting his way in the world, expecting hard knocks and getting them. He is now a man with a long life behind him, notoriously genial of disposition, obviously desiring nothing better than to live at peace with all men, yet compelled in these last years, after heaping up mountains of laborious work and earning a large reputation, to engage in a petty piece of contention with a gentleman of whom no one knows anything outside the little circle of Stratford celebrities. The obvious question is, " why trouble about these people and their doings?" The object . of an attack which (rightly or wrongly) is supposed to carry a charge of grave neglect of a public duty has, however, no choice but to reply. Silence in such a case is too often interpreted unfavourably, and that man is too amiable for an unamiable world who can see without vexation his "benefits forgot." Mr. Halliwell-Phillipps is not concerned to show that Stratford-on-Avon is in his debt; but his friends and the public cannot overlook the gross and manifest ingratitude of the Council, which does not silence at once and emphatically the busybodies who impute, or seem to impute, unworthy transactions to a man who, without pay or fee, at a tangible loss of hard cash to no small amount, and without any earthly realisable or conceivable object other than the public good, has devoted years of work to their service. The tone of speeches made at various times in the Council when proposals of Mr. Halliwell-Phillipps have been discussed, has often been ludicrous enough to any reader possessed of risible faculties at all acute. The Shakespearean scholar offers on one occasion to take the risk of autotyping some Stratford records for sale, the loss, if any, to be his; the profit, if any, to be the Corporation's. The proposal comes up in Council, and Mr. Alderman Bird says "the public would be vastly benefited by the publication." So far well; but presently Sir Arthur Hodgson would like to know if the valuable documents would require to go temporarily out of the possession of the Council. The Mayor replies that that would be a necessity, whereupon Sir Arthur Hodgson warns the Council that if they are of opinion that they "should comply" with Mr. Phillipps's letter—"and he hoped they would do so, for he thought it a very nice one—every care should be taken that the documents should be carefully numbered and registered." The silly farce of such a gracious way of "complying" with an offer to risk a large sum and earn none in the interests of a scheme that would "vastly benefit the public" can only be fully appreciated in the light of the fact that it was Mr. Phillipps himself who told the Council what "value" the documents possessed. But the whole controversy, so far as some of the members of the Stratford Council are concerned, is really too childishly illogical to be seriously considered except so far as it involves a grave offence to an honoured servant, not only of Stratford, but of the greater public. The idea current in the little town that Mr. Phillipps has probably had his *quid pro quo* in the information he has gleaned from the town records ought to be banished by the author's emphatic statement that not nine out of the 700 pages of his "Life of Shakespeare" came out of the documents in dispute. The local press ought really to hold itself superior to such unworthy and palpably erroneous imputations. In dismissing this subject one need only say that the spirit of Mr. Phillipps's farewell to his Stratford friends is everything that could be expected from that most thorough representative of the old style of English gentleman.—*The Liverpool Mercury.*

Mr. J. O. Halliwell-Phillipps has found it necessary to issue a further brochure on "The Stratford Records and the Shakespeare Autotypes." This is intended as "a brief review of singular delusions that are current at Stratford-on-Avon." The pamphlet is by "the supposed delinquent," and his narrative seems to show that he has not been treated with that courtesy and consideration due to him not only as a Shakespearean scholar, but as one who has freely given good time and unpaid service to the Stratford Corporation. Some years ago he offered to arrange and calendar all their documents from the earliest date up to the year 1750, and his offer being gratefully accepted he examined all and arranged 4,869 separate documents, leaving 954 which, as of little interest, were not bound with the others. Since their quarrel with him the Town Council have paid £180 for the arrangement of the four charters and of 119 records of the Guild. If this sum be a proportionate one, it will be seen that Mr. Halliwell-Phillipps's honorary services represent a considerable saving to the town. Early in 1883 he offered to autotype a large number of the Shakespearean records, to bear the loss if any, and in the event of profit resulting to hand it over to the Corporation. As the record-room is too narrow and too badly lighted for photographic purposes, Mr. Halliwell-Phillipps took a single document at a time to the artist's studio, a few hundred yards off, placed it for protection between plates of glass, and as soon as the negative was made returned it to its place in the record-room. There does not appear to be anything very dreadful in this proceeding, and perhaps no one was more astonished than Mr. Halliwell-Phillipps by the censures passed upon him for taking even for such a brief time any document from the record-room, since the discussion in the Town Council on his offer when first made clearly showed that it was understood that the documents would "necessarily" pass into his custody. It is also notable that after objecting to the removal, even for a few moments, of documents from their home at the Birth-Place, the objectors should send 119 documents to London for examination at the Record Office. Yet it has been said that "irregular is the mildest term" for his action! Such is the gist of Mr. Halliwell-Phillipps's latest word on the unpleasant subject of the Stratford records.—*The Manchester Guardian.*

Most of our readers who know anything of Shakespearean literature will be ready to acknowledge their indebtedness

to Mr. J. O. Halliwell-Phillipps, who has devoted himself
for many years to the most minute and painstaking investigation of everything connected with the poet's life and
surroundings. For forty years he has been at work, in
various ways, amongst the Stratford Records. He arranged
and calendared the Corporation Records, without fee or
reward, and his monument is visible in the bound volumes,
containing 4,869 documents, now accessible to the Shakespearean or the antiquary. Two years ago he offered "to
be at the risk "—we quote his own words—"of producing
autotypes of a large number of the Shakespearean town
records, the loss (if any) on the publication to be borne by
myself, the profit (if any) to be handed over to the Corporation." Owing to the discourtesy offered him soon after
he had commenced the undertaking, Mr. Halliwell-Phillipps
has withdrawn from it, and he has now been compelled to
make a defence in a pamphlet which lies before us. We
have not space to describe the events which have produced
estrangement between Mr. Halliwell-Phillipps and the
Corporation, but we must record our opinion, from a full
knowledge of the nature of his services to the town, and
to world-wide students of Shakespeare, that Mr. Halliwell-
Phillipps has been treated with unpardonable rudeness,
suspicion, and want of consideration. The whole Corporation is, happily, not to blame, but that is, as far as Mr.
Halliwell-Phillipps and the general public are concerned, a
small matter. At great personal labour and expense he has
devoted himself to a task no other man could have done
so well, and to offer him discourtesy, after so many years, is
a reproach to the town, and calls for the remonstrance of
all who venerate our national poet, and sympathise with an
honourable and high-minded man in what has been a long
mission of toil and labour in the service of literature.—
York Herald.

Mr. Halliwell-Phillipps has printed for circulation among
his friends a dignified remonstrance against the discourtesy
with which he has been treated by Mr. C. Flower, of
Stratford-on-Avon, after having gratuitously calendared all

the ancient charters and other documents belonging to that ancient town in which rest the bones of Shakespeare. He also protests, and most justly, against a statement in the Stratford Herald to the effect that he allowed valuable papers entrusted to his charge to lie about "unclassified, uncalendared, and uncared for"—the real fact being, as he clearly shows, that he recommended to the Mayor and Corporation to bind such, and such only, as were of real historic value ; he also states that while Mr. Flower reflected on him for taking valuable documents to a house a few yards off, to be reproduced by the autotype process, the same Mr. Flower felt no scruple in sending up to London 119 records, and leaving them there for several months !—*The Antiquarian Magazine.*

We have received "The Stratford Records and the Shakespeare Autotypes : a Brief Review of Singular Delusions that are current at Stafford-upon-Avon," by the Supposed Delinquent, third edition (Brighton). It gives a denial by our valued contributor, Mr. Halliwell-Phillipps, of charges, real or supposed, of neglect in the discharge of his voluntary functions in regard to the Stratford-on-Avon records. No one who knows the zealous, loyal, painstaking, and self-denying services Mr. Halliwell-Phillipps has rendered to everything connected with Stratford-upon-Avon, its documents included, can believe that any justification can be necessary. With regard to a matter that has approached unpleasantly near a quarrel, we will only say that this seems emphatically a case in which friendly arbitration should put an end to difficulties. That Mr. Halliwell-Phillipps has what seems a perfect vindication needs not be said. The only surprise is that anything capable of being supposed to be an implication of carelessness could ever have appeared to be brought against him.—*Notes and Queries.*

Mr. Halliwell-Phillipps has issued a brief review of what he calls the "Singular Delusions that are current at Stratford-upon-Avon." That the charges of "neglect" and "irregularity" which have been preferred by influential members of the Town Council, and repeated elsewhere, are here satisfactorily disposed of, we need hardly say. Considering how deeply the town is indebted to the disinterested services of this enthusiastic scholar, the pamphlet nevertheless leaves a painful impression.—*The Daily News.*

The tempest aroused by the recent attacks upon Mr. J. O. Halliwell-Phillipps concerning his relations with Stratford-on-Avon has by no means subsided, as his latest pamphlet clearly shows. The first edition was so masterly a defence that anything further seemed uncalled for. Yet not only has Mr. Halliwell-Phillipps's explanation not been accepted, as it should have been, but renewed attacks have been made upon him both by the Stratford papers and by Mr. Charles Flower, who has taken so prominent a part in the matter. The difficulty between Mr. Halliwell-Phillipps and the Corporation had been disposed of by a resolution passed by the latter on January 4th, in which they complimented him on the value of his work and invited him to continue it. Accepting this resolution in the spirit in which it originated Mr. Halliwell-Phillipps prepared to continue his work, and even expressed his willingness to do so with the conjunction of a committee, although he had always objected to such an arrangement. Yet scarcely had he renewed his labour when he learned that Mr. Charles Flower was operating against him in another quarter, and while it was a matter outside the Corporation, the nature of the case was such as would not permit of the two working together. Mr. Halliwell-Phillipps has, therefore, announced that his connection with Stratford-on-Avon has ceased, a conclusion to be regretted, not only that so eminent a student should have met with difficulties and unkindness in the prosecution of his labours, but also because his opponents, instead of destroying his defence, are only satisfied with heaping additional abuse upon his head.—*The United States Shakespeareana.*

LONDON:

HARRISON AND SONS, PRINTERS IN ORDINARY TO HER MAJESTY,
ST. MARTIN'S LANE.